STORM DAMAGE

Guy Devereau erupts into Poppy's life one stormy night. The power lines come down, it is freezing cold and, delirious, Guy hauls her into his bed. How better to obey doctor's orders to keep him warm? The following morning, Poppy discovers that Guy is the absentee landlord who wants her to vacate the cottage, and also that he has forgotten about the previous night. How can she remind him, especially when the glamorous Nerissa turns up to claim him?

SPECIAL MESSAGE TO READERS

This book is published under the auspices of

THE ULVERSCROFT FOUNDATION
(registered charity No. 264873 UK)

Established in 1972 to provide funds for
research, diagnosis and treatment of eye diseases.
Examples of contributions made are: —

A new Children's Assessment Unit at
Moorfield's Hospital, London.

•

Twin operating theatres at the
Western Ophthalmic Hospital, London.

•

A Chair of Ophthalmology at the
University of Leicester.

•

The establishment of a Royal Australian College
of Ophthalmologists "Fellowship".

You can help further the work of the Foundation
by making a donation or leaving a legacy. Every
contribution, no matter how small, is received
with gratitude. Please write for details to:

THE ULVERSCROFT FOUNDATION,
The Green, Bradgate Road, Anstey,
Leicester LE7 7FU, England.
Telephone: (0116) 236 4325

In Australia write to:
THE ULVERSCROFT FOUNDATION,
c/o The Royal Australian College of
Ophthalmologists,
27, Commonwealth Street, Sydney,
N.S.W. 2010.

LORNA McKENZIE

◆

STORM DAMAGE

Complete and Unabridged

LINFORD
Leicester

First published in Great Britain in 1993 by
Robert Hale Limited
London

First Linford Edition
published July 1995
by arrangement with
Robert Hale Limited
London

British Library CIP Data

McKenzie, Lorna
    Storm damage.—Large print ed.—
    Linford romance library
    I. Title II. Series
    823.914 [F]

    ISBN 0-7089-7739-1

Published by
F. A. Thorpe (Publishing) Ltd.
Anstey, Leicestershire

Set by Words & Graphics Ltd.
Anstey, Leicestershire
Printed and bound in Great Britain by
T. J. Press (Padstow) Ltd., Padstow, Cornwall

This book is printed on acid-free paper

1

IT was a wild night — and a cold one.

Poppy Winters pulled on a stylish cream sweater, patterned with coppery autumn leaves. It was one of her own designs, and exactly right with her cream shirt and cords. It was also, though she didn't realize it, a perfect foil for her wavy chestnut hair and pale camellia-like skin. She glanced in the wardrobe mirror, wide green eyes, usually sparkling with *joie de vivre* glared back, dark with fury.

Who did they think they were, these London solicitors, agents for the Devereau estate? What if the Devereau family could trace its ancestry back to the Norman conquest! She, Poppy Winters, had been born in this Dorset cottage. Her father, like his father and grandfather before him, had lived and worked as head gardeners on the Devereau estate all their lives. Whereas the present owner of Cranford Hall had first seen the light of day in far-flung Australia, and there he would have remained but for his distant cousin, the recently deceased Percy Hugh Devereau, having the ill grace to die without a son and heir.

Now, apparently, he — the Australian beneficiary — was coming to claim his inheritance and move into the Hall. As a result Poppy's cottage was required for his new head gardener, as yet to be appointed, to tame the jungle resulting from a whole year's neglect — since Poppy's father had died, in fact.

Poppy skipped down the enclosed staircase into her cosy sitting-room where logs burned merrily in the ingle-nook fireplace, sending out a wonderful heat. Going through to her tiny but neat kitchen she picked up the supper tray she had already prepared, with a bowl of home-made soup, a boiled egg and an orange, and returned to the fireside to eat. As she did so, she picked up the letter again to study its stark black and white phrases.

The arrival of the new owner being imminent — in two weeks' time it was mooted in the village — *it would be appreciated if you could vacate the cottage without the statutory month's notice, and accept one month's rent in lieu. We understand you have no dependants so you will doubtless appreciate this opportunity to move to a younger, more go-ahead city environment.*

"Like hell I would!" she stormed aloud.

The only answer was the wind, finding its way through every tiny crevice, rattling the windows in their frames, slamming against the sturdy front door and howling down the chimney to suck up flame and sparks and send occasional flurries of smoke into the room.

Well, they'd got another think coming! She had a right to stay here! Her father had been both gardener and handyman at the Hall, besides being a superb craftsman, making exquisite wood-carvings in his spare time. Her mother had been housekeeper and seamstress for the late Percy Hugh, and had stitched beautiful *petit point* pictures as a hobby. Their artistic streak had emerged in Poppy, after a stint at art college, in a flair for knitwear design. She bought her yarns locally, and dyed them in the wash-house attached to the cottage, using natural dyes from garden and hedgerow. Just the sort of thing you'd find in your smart, city environment!

What was she to do though? Fate had dealt her several cruel blows: first her mother had died after a lengthy battle against cancer, then her father, two months later, of a heart attack, brought on, Poppy was sure, by grief. Now, this.

With fluid grace she stood up and went to peer out at the October night. The moon, clad in drifting veils of black, disappeared behind one of the heavy masses of cloud that floated in ghostly procession across the stormy sky. Strong gusts of wind buffeted everything in their path, bending the black outlines of some of the sturdiest trees, and lifting unsecured items to toss around like flotsam.

There goes the dustbin, Poppy groaned, as something landed with a metallic clang, followed by rhythmic rocking movements like those of some crazy diabolo.

At the top of a slope, some quarter of a mile away, stood the solid outline of Cranford Hall, harshly silhouetted against the stormy backcloth of night.

Letting the curtain fall Poppy switched on the television in time for the final news headlines: another shooting in Belfast, a political scandal in France, more regional demonstrations in Russia, a worrying situation in the Middle East. Finally, the weather forecast.

"A storm warning is issued for . . . "

Everything went black, and silent. There was just the glow of the fire to light the room, the rhythmic tick-tick of the mantel clock to be heard inside, while outside the storm raged unabated.

The power-lines were down — a not uncommon occurence in this locality. Poppy soon unearthed and lit some candles, a necessity she always kept handy. That done, the room looked cosy and almost Victorian, with just the candle-light and a crackling fire. Luckily she had the ancient Aga on which to make her coffee.

She was just sipping the hot brew and, unavoidably, listening to the storm blustering outside when, above the noise of the wind, buffeting the flint and brick cottage, came a crashing, almighty thud.

Christ! What was that?

With nothing to do but fret, Poppy, not normally a nervous person, debated whether to sit tight and wait for the storm to pass, or venture out to investigate the provenance of that crash. She was half out of her chair, having decided on the latter, rather than do nothing, when she thought she heard a knock at her door.

Who on earth would come calling at this hour? Her nerves must be playing tricks. The house stood on the edge of the village, with only the back lane to the Hall running beside it, itself a turning off the main village street. She must have imagined it. No, there it was again, a definite, insistent hammering.

It was something she had always dreaded — an unknown caller after dark. If only she had a dog! Or a gun — even a toy replica! She had always meant to get a door-chain fixed — the poker! That would be the best weapon, in case whoever it was was calling with evil intent.

It was probably some stranded motorist who had strayed off the road in search of a garage. Nevertheless, she armed herself with the sturdy brass poker before leaving the sitting-room.

She stood quaking, undecided, in her small, square hall, little larger than a cupboard, when whoever-it-was chose that moment to seize the knocker to deal further punishing blows to her door.

She grasped the doorknob, turned it and pulled, opening the door with a flourish, while brandishing the poker in her other hand. Whoever-it-was crashed inside, bringing with him a fair portion of howling gale, lashing rain and swirling autumn leaves. She felt as though she had been charged by an elephant as her caller stumbled wetly into her, dashing the poker to the ground, before turning to close the door. Despite his size he was having considerable difficulty in doing so against the force of the wind. Instinctively Poppy joined her meagre strength to his and together they managed it. He then picked up the fallen poker and, with a courteous nod, handed it back, making her feel thoroughly foolish. His bulk filled the small, shadowy space and she stepped backwards, pushing wide the inner door to the sitting-room. He exuded an aura of potent masculinity and she felt an urgent need to put some space between them.

"C-come in," she invited. "I'm afraid the power's off, but at least there's candle-light in here."

He stood in the middle of the room, breathing hard. In what light there was she took a closer look at him. His coal black hair, flattened by rain, was dripping onto the collar of a green Barbour jacket. Khaki cords tucked into studded green wellingtons clung wetly to long, muscled thighs. Candle-light glowed in amazing, light hazel eyes fringed with thick black lashes, now wetly gummed together. He was handsome in a harsh, uncompromising way, his bone structure strong, his brown cheeks lean. Only the curving lines of his lips suggested something softer, more sensual in his nature. She peered more closely at the rain trickling down the grooves of his face.

On the right side, she quickly discovered, it wasn't rain at all — it was blood!

"You're hurt!" she exclaimed. "What happened?"

She now noticed a certain glazed puzzlement in his extraordinarily beautiful eyes.

"A tree crashed down on my Range Rover."

"That must have been the noise I heard! My God, it fell on *you*! Can I take a look?"

With shaky fingers she reached up and lifted a lock of black hair that had fallen forward. There was a nasty gash across his temple.

"Will I live?" he asked wryly.

"Probably," she told him with a hint of mischief. "I think you ought to see a doctor, though, as soon as possible. I'll call him."

She was soon through, explaining to Dr Wilson what had happened.

"There's no way I can get to you

tonight," he told her regretfully. "Every road hereabouts is blocked by fallen trees. It's a good sign, though, if he's talking lucidly. Clean up the wound, keep him warm and comfortable, and call me in the morning. If you're worried during the night, I'll advise over the phone. Don't hesitate to . . . "

The line went dead, and Poppy was alone with her unknown caller.

"He says you'll be just fine," she assured him cheerfully. "You just need to stay warm and comfortable till the farmers can clear the fallen trees and Doctor Wilson can get through. You'd better get out of that wet gear. I'm Poppy Winters, by the way."

He nodded fractionally, his features contracting as if in pain.

"Do you have a headache?"

"The mother and father of one. Have you any painkillers?"

She did, but should he be taking anything? At the moment he was having difficulty getting his jacket off.

"Let me help you," she offered.

She slid the jacket from his shoulders, which were so wide they needed no padding to enhance them, and then urged him to sit near the fire while she removed his boots. That done, she sat back on her heels and looked up at him.

"Are you hungry?" she asked.

"No, I ate . . . " he waved a hand vaguely, " . . . somewhere on the road."

He fell silent and leaned his head against the back of the chair, looking down at her through lowered lashes as if seeing her for the first time. Despite his obvious pain, in his eyes she discerned a masculine appreciation of her vibrant colouring and soft curvy body in the autumnal sweater and well-fitting cords. Her heart began to pound unnaturally fast within her breast. He was the most attractive man she had ever set eyes on and just looking at him caused a strange, alien fluttering at the pit of her stomach.

"Can I get you some coffee?" Her

voice emerged maddeningly husky.

"How about a stiff whisky?"

His was equally soft. Well, why not?

She returned with his drink and a bowl of antiseptic. He accepted the whisky gratefully and downed it in one. Settling on an upright chair beside him she proceeded to clean the wound. The gash was not deep but he had taken a hard knock — he'd have a terrific bruise in the morning. She held away a lock of dark, silky hair while she tended the cut; her fingertips wanted to stroke the line of a glossy black brow, as dark as his incredibly long lashes. He glanced up, turning his warm, golden gaze on her as if to commit to memory the wide green eyes, small straight nose, curvy, generous mouth, and shiny tumble of chestnut hair caught up carelessly on one side.

As she worked, she recalled Dr Wilson's words. He had told her to keep him warm till morning so he was taking it for granted that the man would stay here. And she could hardly turn him out — it would be inhuman on such a night, and where could he go?

"I-it looks as though you're stuck here till morning," she told him and, remembering the kettle of hot water on the Aga: "I'll put a hot-water bottle in the bed in my parents' room — the guest-room, I should say."

She escaped to perform the task and gather her wits together.

"Where are your parents?" he enquired on her return.

"I'm afraid they're both dead. It was not that long ago, so I still think of the room as theirs. Oh, they didn't actually die in there."

She didn't know why she was telling him that. He didn't look the sort of man to be scared of ghosts — or anything else for that matter.

He set down his empty glass and leaned back, wearily closing his eyes. He mustn't fall asleep here — the room became chilly at night, and she didn't fancy getting up every couple of hours to stoke the fire.

"Would you like another drink?" she asked.

He half opened his eyes. "Mm-mm," he grunted negatively.

"You really should go up to bed," she said gently. "There's a portable gas lamp in the kitchen. I'll light it for you."

Perhaps she shouldn't have given him that drink. His eyes looked more glazed and distant now — she would hate to have his death on her hands! She fetched the lamp.

Reaction at last! He leaned forwards and tried to stand up. He stumbled, but she was there beside him, supporting him as best she could — he was no lightweight.

"It's this way." She guided him towards the enclosed stairs and then slowly upwards, step by step, holding the lamp in her free hand. "The bathroom's in there, and this is your room. I'll find you a robe, and some pyjamas . . . "

This brought his head swivelling to

hers. "Pyjamas?" There was even the glimmer of a smile.

"Okay, okay, so you sleep in the raw. Me too, but in case . . . "

She fell silent, turning scarlet at the admission she had just made. A good thing the man was almost *non compos mentis*!

He collapsed on the edge of the bed, bringing her down beside him. She extricated herself, found a robe which had belonged to her father, and hastened to the door where she paused.

"Can I get you anything else, Mr . . . ?"

"You could run me a bath."

She shrugged, surprised that in his state he wanted to bother, but complied anyway, standing the lamp on a Victorian chest on the landing where spare towels were stored, relieved to escape his ambience that both compelled and threatened. Once the bath was full she turned the taps off, and straightened to find him just

16

behind her. She stepped away smartly, annoyed by the smile that played about his mouth.

He threw the bathrobe over a chair and started unfastening his shirt, seemingly unconcerned by her presence — he had already discarded his sweater. The shirt fell to the ground and she stared in wide-eyed fascination at his huge shoulders and wide, muscled chest with its dark coating of hair. Shaking herself mentally, she thrust a bath-sheet and a toothbrush still in its wrapper into his hands, set the lamp down and left, closing the door behind her.

Downstairs she tidied up and made the fire safe, then went back upstairs, using a candle this time to light her way. She could hear nothing — suppose he had fainted in the bath? Oh God, there were times like these when she fervently wished she did live in the middle of town.

Times like these? What was she thinking about? When had times ever been like these, with a total stranger lying in her bath, in heaven only knew what mental state? Yet irrationally she felt no fear. As she reached the landing she heard the sound of a large body raising itself from the bath. She listened for a few seconds more, heard a couple of grunts and the odd oath then, deciding it was safe to leave him to his own devices, she went to her room and shut the door.

She had showered earlier so now she merely cleaned off her make-up as best she could by the light of her candle, and started brushing her hair. There was something definitely alluring about candle-light, she decided. No wonder the Victorians weren't too bothered about make-up. This gentle glow didn't rob the complexion of its natural colour as electricity did. Her hair tumbled in gleaming chestnut ripples about her face. She'd have to do her teeth when *he* had finished in there. Meanwhile she might as well undress.

She folded her sweater neatly, placed her cord trousers over a chair and removed her underwear. She dropped this into her linen bin and was reaching for her robe when the door opened.

"Get out!" she yelled, clutching the robe to hide her curvy slenderness, her eyes wide with horror at the huge man standing in her doorway, looking shocked and rather confused.

"Sorry, wrong room," he mumbled, and left, quietly closing the door.

But not before he had glanced beyond her, she now realized, where the mirror offered a perfect rear view of herself. As she climbed into bed a little later, she was still suffering from a racing pulse in the knowledge that his brief visual inspection had not been entirely unpleasant. The wind continued pounding the cottage, though with slightly less vigour, as through sheer exhaustion Poppy fell asleep.

A strange sound woke her. She groped around for the light switch, and when it didn't work, she remembered the events of the night before. Lighting the candle proved difficult in the dark, but she finally managed it. Her bedside clock showed half-past one. She listened intently.

There it was again: her uninvited guest groaning in his sleep. What should she do? She'd better investigate.

She set down her candle on a chest opposite his bed, so that its light shone through the brass rails at the foot to reveal its occupant, threshing about wildly. His brow was beaded with sweat. She felt her way downstairs and returned with a glass of water.

"Here, drink this," she urged him, putting an arm under his shoulders to help him sit up.

He looked at her with bleary eyes but did as she asked. She put the glass down.

"You were having a nightmare. Should I get you a couple of aspirins?"

"No." His hand fell over hers where it lay on the coverlet. "Sorry I'm such a nuisance . . . " he lifted his eyes to look straight into hers, "Poppy," he finished.

At least he remembered her name. His hand felt good over hers but she thought it wise to extricate herself. His deeply tanned shoulders against the stark white pillows were doing something to her pulse rate. A shudder shook his body.

"Jeez, it's cold," he said, his teeth chattering.

"I'm afraid I don't have central heating and the power's still off."

He released her hand and slid under the covers. A huge shudder shook his body. And another. Keep him warm, the doctor had said. He started groaning again and threshing about. When he turned her way again his eyes were unseeing, delirious. He shot an arm out and, before she could resist, scooped her into bed beside him, holding her tightly against his shaking body. What was she to do? Perhaps if she were to stay for just a moment just till he warmed up . . .

Easing her robe carefully about her to form a barrier between them, she lay rigidly against him. They could sleep back to back, she decided, but when she turned he merely drew her into the curve of his body. Gradually his shivers subsided and she was sure he was asleep. Should she leave? She had never before slept in a man's arms — it was heaven. She thought of her own cold, unwelcoming bed and snuggled closer and soon she too was asleep.

It was still dark when she drifted into a half-dreaming state. Her robe had become disentangled from her body. She felt warm and wonderful, without that painful loneliness that haunted the long, dark nights. She snuggled closer to the source of warmth.

She sighed softly as a melting heat suffused her, gasping at sweet, unfamiliar sensations. What a heavenly dream!

At some point pain intruded but it quickly subsided, to be replaced by such sweet warmth and satisfaction she never wanted to awake.

But she did, to discover that it

had been no dream — the handsome stranger was slumped by her side, his gentle, regular breathing telling her he was asleep. Carefully she slid out of bed and took herself off to her own room, where she lay for a long time asking herself over and over again: 'What have I *done*? What *have* I done?'

Dawn was peering over the eastern horizon when Poppy next awoke. She ached in every muscle, and in muscles of which she had hitherto been unaware. What on earth . . . then it all came back with a rush, and she flushed hotly with shame, yet mingled with an aching need to be back in the strangers arms.

Well, she couldn't just lie here all day. She had to face him some time. Nevertheless, she delayed the moment as long as possible, creeping about the place as she showered and went down to tidy up, clear out the ashes and relay the fire. That done, she made a pot of coffee.

What if he preferred tea? Oh, what was wrong with her? He was lucky to get anything! He'd already had a bed for the night, her tender, loving care — *and* the precious gift she had sworn to save for the man she married, until now a vague, shadowy creature without substance. Now, a total stranger had become her first lover.

She was halfway up the stairs when the landing light sprang on — she must have switched in on automatically last night. Now the power had been restored. Marvellous! At least some things were getting back to normal! The phone was still dead though, when she checked for dialling tone.

Outside the door of the guest-room she stood for a long moment and then knocked timidly. No response. She knocked again, then pushed the door wide and walked in. The light from the landing fell on the man in bed, who immediately put up a hand to shield his eyes.

"What the . . . who . . . where am I?

What the devil am I doing here? And who the blazes are you?"

With a sinking feeling Poppy set the cup down and went round the bed to draw back the curtains. She felt deep hurt and rejection, but at least there was no need to feel embarrassed — he hadn't a clue who she was!

She took a deep breath. "What shall I answer first?" she enquired. "You're in Briar Cottage which stands in the lane leading to a place called Cranford Hall . . . "

He raised himself in bed to pick up his coffee; his eyes now swivelled to her. "I'm near Cranford Hall? Good God! I must have had a skinful last night! I don't remember getting here. D-did we meet in a pub?"

"Secondly," she went on, ignoring his assumption — only too correct! — of what had passed between them, "you had a slight contretemps with a tree and cut your head."

He lifted a hand, tentatively seeking his injury, and settling almost at once on the gash on his temple.

"I hit a tree? In my new Range Rover? Christ!"

"No, it was the other way round, actually!"

He gave her a narrowed stare. "Okay, cut the sarcasm and corny jokes!"

"It happens to be true," she persisted. "There was quite a storm last night — trees falling like nine-pins all over the place, apparently." Well, Dr Wilson had said all the roads were blocked! "One chose to topple on your car, you stumbled in here and the doctor, when I rang him, suggested . . . suggested that you stay here till he could get through this morning."

"Oh Lord, I suppose I owe you an apology — that bit about the pub."

Which was as near as he got to giving one.

"Lastly — in case you've forgotten — I'm Poppy Winters."

"Poppy? What sort of a name is that? Poppy." He said the name as if he were savouring it — he obviously had no recollection of her at all. "The red hair, I suppose."

"I was practically bald till my first birthday! No, my parents just liked the name."

"Winters — now that rings a bell." Golden eyes narrowed suspiciously. "My agents were anticipating some trouble with a Miss Winters . . . "

"*Your* agents? Just who are you?" she demanded, now more than a little suspicious herself.

"Guy Devereau — nice to meet you, Poppy."

2

H E sat up straight and offered his hand — which she declined. Things fell rapidly into place: the reason he had been in the lane to the Hall at that time of night; his deep, practically all-over tan — from living in Australia; his arrogance this morning on waking up.

"I'll leave you to get dressed," she said coldly, turning away and making for the door.

"Poppy! Come back here! Why the devil are you acting like that?"

"I'd rather talk downstairs when you're dressed."

"What makes you think I'm fit to get up? Poppy, I said come back here!"

She looked back. He was half out of bed, the covers somewhere round his hips.

"I'd rather talk later, if you don't mind," she said quietly.

"Does the sight of my body offend you?" He paused. "How did I get undressed — didn't you help me?"

"Only with your jacket and boots! Would you like some breakfast?"

"In bed?"

A corner of his mouth lifted in a half smile.

"No! You used the blue toothbrush last night, and there are disposable razors in the cabinet. I'll put out a clean towel."

"What an efficient little soul!"

"Don't patronize me, Mr Devereau," she snapped, closing the door a little too firmly as she left.

She set a plate of bacon, eggs and mushrooms in front of him when he appeared, washed and dressed, in the kitchen.

"The phone's back on and the doctor's on his way," she informed him. "The farmer's men have cleared all the local roads of fallen trees, and they're towing your Range Rover to the Hall as it's new, they thought you'd want to make arrangements other than the local garage."

"Thanks. Sorry the bed's so mussed up — I must have been pretty restless in the night . . . "

Poppy turned away quickly. He had no recollection whatever of what had passed between them, and now she could never tell him. She had allowed her worst enemy — the man who wanted to deprive her of her lifelong home, her base, her place of work — to make love to her. And he couldn't even remember!

"You were feverish," she told him, putting her own plate on the table. "More coffee?"

If his appetite was any guide, he had certainly recovered. He emptied his plate and filled up with several slices of toast and marmalade, after which he poured them some more coffee from the pot standing on the Aga, and sat down again.

"Now then, Poppy, what's the score?"

"Wh-what do you mean?"

"You changed from a ministering angel to a tight-lipped virago at the mention of my name."

"And you really don't know why, Mr Devereau?"

"And what's with the Mr Devereau? After your generous hospitality, can't you call me Guy?"

"It was, as you say, just a night's hospitality — would you have accepted, if you knew your agents had served me notice to quit?"

"So that's the way the land lies! I'll look into it — I've had to leave everything to agents so far. Is there any special reason you're attached to this cottage?"

"Every reason!" she stormed. "I was born here, I've lived here all my life, my friends are here, my work is here . . ."

"Work? What kind of work?"

"I suppose you could call it a cottage industry," she said wryly. "I design and sell sweaters."

"Is that one of your designs?"

He indicated the one she was wearing — her autumn leaves again.

"Yes, it is."

"Very nice, too." His gaze wandered somewhat personally over the sweater, bringing a flush to her cheeks. Damn the man! "But you could do that anywhere, couldn't you?"

"No, I couldn't!" she said heatedly. "I make my own dyes from plants gathered locally, and others grown specially. So no, I couldn't do it anywhere."

"Well, it surely doesn't have to be this particular cottage!"

"It does! It's got all the facilities I need. And I don't intend to move!"

"Well, I've bloody well moved halfway round the world to live in this cold, windy, God-forsaken place. I'm only asking you to move from this particular cottage. You needn't even leave the village."

It had never occurred to her that

he might be a reluctant heir. Nevertheless . . .

"Have you any idea how much little
rustic dwellings cost these days? Young
people can't afford to live in the villages
they were born in! Labourers' cottages
are being tarted up and sold as bijou
residences to yuppies, or the wealthy
retired. Is that what . . . ?"

"That's not what I'm proposing. I'll
have to consult my agents. Look, I've
got a stinking headache could we
postpone this discussion to another
time?"

"All right," she agreed grudgingly.
"Would you like an aspirin? Oh, here's
Dr Wilson."

She saw Robin pass the window
with some relief. He had only been
in practice with his father for two
years. Like Poppy he had been born
in the village. He was, at thirty, six
years older than Poppy, but she had
known him, man and boy, all her
life, played tennis with him at the
local tennis club, danced with him at

church socials, acted with him in the drama group . . .

"Hello, Poppy, how's my prettiest patient?"

"Your patient is not particularly pretty," she informed him acidly, indicating the scowling figure of Guy Devereau. "This is Mr Devereau, who didn't quite make it to the Hall last night . . . "

"Lucky man — I've been trying for years to be invited here for breakfast!"

It wasn't true. Robin, despite his casual, boyish charm, was an excellent doctor, and had never been more than a friend — one of a group of friends. More like a brother, in fact.

"It certainly gives a new meaning to bedside manner," Guy commented drily. "Good morning, Dr Wilson."

"Call me Robin. Everyone thinks of my father as Dr Wilson. He's Poppy's doctor, actually — she and I are just good friends."

Guy gave her another narrow-eyed look as Robin busied himself setting his bag down on a counter.

"Perhaps you'd like to use the sitting-room," Poppy suggested. "I have one or two things to do."

By the time she returned from upstairs her laundry basket was full and there wasn't a trace to remind her of the previous night. Her parents' room was restored to its neat and tidy state, cleaned and dusted with the bed made up anew.

"He'll live," Robin declared when she reappeared.

"Good," she said absently. "Coffee, Robin?"

"No, thanks all the same, Poppy. Must dash — I'm taking surgery this morning. Nice to have met you, Guy. I'll look in at the Hall in a couple of days. By then you'll probably have perfect recall of what happened in those lost hours. Unless it's something your subconscious would prefer to forget! Just think," he gave them both a broad grin: "Anything might have happened!"

Thanks for nothing, Robin, Poppy

seethed inwardly. I'll just die if he ever remembers. Let sleeping dogs lie, likewise forgotten love — or whatever it might more appropriately be called.

"He's a nice bloke, Robin," Guy conceded, when they were alone. "I'm joining him in a round of golf on Sunday morning, before church. Meanwhile, I'd better go and inspect my new home before I talk to lawyers and accountants."

He put a hand to his brow, closing his eyes briefly.

"Your head still hurts, doesn't it?" she guessed. He nodded stiffly. "You'd do better to take yourself off to bed for a day or so till you feel better."

He turned to look at her across the metre separating them.

"Will you come and tuck me in?" he enquired indolently.

She tossed her red hair angrily and turned away. "No, I damn well won't! You'd probably arrange for the bailiffs to call while I was away!"

He chuckled and she glanced up,

arrested despite herself by the gleaming white teeth cutting a white slash through his handsome features. The smile lit up his whole face and turned his amber eyes to gold. To her alarm he reached out, twisted a skein of her hair round his fingers, and tugged her gently towards him. He inspected the coiled strand closely.

"Amazing colour!" he breathed. "Seems it's true, too — it really does go with a sparky temperament."

"Let me go," she said, twisting her neck to reclaim her hair.

Instead of obliging he stepped towards her, his other hand tilting her chin till her eyes met his. "Did anyone ever tell you your eyes are like emeralds?" he murmured. "Especially when the tears aren't far away — like now. Why, Poppy?"

"You're wrong — I just got a grain or two of dust in my eyes while I was cleaning."

"Thanks for being so neighbourly last night," he said softly, and bent to touch his lips to hers.

She should have pulled away but instead she returned the pressure of his lips. His gentle touch was all it took to spark off pulsing sensations along nerves which had been newly awakened a few short hours ago, and set her blood pounding thickly through her veins. Her arms were soon clinging round his neck. He drew away, his expression almost shocked.

"Hey, cool it, Poppy — I'm the one doing the thanking."

"Automatic reaction," she muttered. "I guess you're pretty experienced."

"Seems that makes two of us," he returned grimly.

"You're wrong!" she declared hotly. "Now get out!"

"Ma'am," he replied, doffing an imaginary cap.

She supposed she should have offered to run him up the lane in her ancient 2CV, but perhaps the walk would cool him down. No, *she* was the one who needed cooling down. Oh, God!

Until lunch-time she threw herself into a frenzy of cleaning, then after a light salad she set to work on her knitting-machine, concentrating hard on the intricate pattern she was weaving. The sweater was almost finished so she carried on till the light began to fade, just managing to complete the last section of ribbing before she had to give up.

She was drawing the curtains in her sitting-room when she paused and glanced up the lane towards the Hall. It was ablaze with light, and she wondered how Guy was coping up there all alone. In Percy Hugh's day, her father would have been in the grounds most of the day, organizing the small team of gardeners who had kept lawns and flower-beds well tended and the kitchen-garden productive all year round. Her mother would have been inside, keeping the food stores well-stocked and the place immaculate, when she wasn't engaged in repairing rare tapestries or precious embroideries.

There had been a team of cleaners to look after the domestic side of things.

No wonder Percy Hugh had never felt the need of a wife! There had been rumours of a well-kept lady in some chic London apartment, but the Hall had been his private domain. A pity he hadn't married and produced an heir, then Poppy wouldn't have met the arrogant new owner, nor be facing the prospect of homelessness.

This wasn't the only cottage on the estate, after all. There were at least three empty ones on the other side of the Hall. Let the new gardener live in one of those! They had stood empty for several years: a positive disgrace, many locals declared, to allow perfectly sound cottages to fall into disrepair, in these days of housing shortages. Let Guy Devereau repair those!

What would he be doing about supper tonight? She reached for the phone. No, she couldn't phone him — he thought her a brazen enough hussy as it was. But she couldn't let him starve, and he was in no fit state to look after himself. She reached again for the phone but, before she could lift it, it rang.

"Poppy?"

"Oh, hello, Esther," she said, relieved to hear the homely voice of Robin's mother. She had been like a second mother to Poppy since her parents had died. "How are you? Did you survive the storm intact?"

Not a good choice of word, she thought wryly, hoping Esther would not enquire the same of herself.

"We lost a couple of slates, otherwise we're fine, but I gather you had a spot of excitement at the height of the storm!"

"You could say that."

"Robin says he's a decent sort of bloke, this Guy Devereau. I've invited him to dinner, and thought you might like to come along, too."

"Oh, I was just going to have a quiet supper by the fire . . . "

"You get enough of those. Come

on, love, the poor man doesn't know anyone else round here, and with Tess away, there aren't many pretty young things to grace our table. We've invited the God squad from the vicarage, but what with Desmond's sleazy stories and Madge's aimless prattle, not to mention daughter Annabel's predatory antics, we'd like someone sane along, too."

"Oh, all right, you've twisted my arm . . . not that I feel particularly sane, mind you."

"Anything to do with Guy Devereau? Robin said he's not bad looking, which probably means he's pretty stunning!"

"It's nothing to do with his looks, Esther — though he's handsome enough. But yes, it is to do with him, and the fact that he wants me out, to make room for his new staff."

"Oh dear! Robin said he seemed to have got under your skin. Oh dear, I'd no idea . . . "

"Don't worry, Esther." She could imagine poor, caring Esther desperately wanting to withdraw Guy's invitation.

"I promise not to make a scene or embarrass you in any way."

She did, however, take tremendous trouble with her appearance that evening. After wearing sensible country clothes during the day, dinner parties offered a chance to dress up, and she and her friends generally did. Besides, some little voice suggested, Annabel would be there, doing her best to seduce every attractive man in sight, which meant Robin and Guy. Annabel was not the typical vicar's daughter but then, neither was her father the typical vicar: away from the pulpit his stories veered towards the suggestive. These, fortunately, went over the head of his scatty wife, Madge, who was a bishop's daughter. She was the only typical member of their household, in fact. Her life consisted of charitable work for the less fortunate, whether they required it or not.

Poppy was glad she had worn her cream silk. Its soft satiny folds draped about her body, offering subtle hints of the curves beneath, rather than making a bold statement. The cowl neck scooped low at the back, while the front sported a keyhole effect giving a tantalizing glimpse of cleavage; the skirt rippled about her slender hips as she moved. Her make-up was equally subtle and her hair, like polished chestnuts and the only vibrant colour about her, was dressed high on her crown, leaving a few stray curls about her slender neck. Long pendant earrings drew further attention to its graceful length. Compared with Annabel, Poppy looked positively fragile. Annabel's black hair was a ragged, backcombed halo about a heavily made-up face: her sequinned top clung, while her tight black skirt must surely be uncomfortable to sit in.

Whatever Esther's misgivings they hadn't prevented her seating Guy next to Poppy. Guy leaned towards her over the melon cocktail.

"You don't fool me, Poppy Winters. There's a core of steel under that delicate exterior."

"Wh-what? Look, if you're going to sit there and insult me all evening, I suggest we change places right now. I'll say it's draughty here . . . "

"You'll do no such thing. I might get landed with Jezebel!"

"She's only a vicar's daughter," said Poppy coyly, her eyes sparkling wickedly.

"Yes, and there are several endings to that little quip! Most of which could well be appropriate."

Poppy gave a little chuckle.

"No private jokes now," Vicar Desmond admonished.

"I suppose after spending a night under the same roof, they've got a lot to talk about!" declared Annabel with a pout, her dark eyes casting daggers in Poppy's direction.

"I'm hoping she'll tell me about it," Guy replied, giving Annabel a devastating smile which banished her peevish expression.

"You poor man, losing your memory like that," put in Madge. "If there's anything we can do, we're always there to help."

"I'll remember that."

The conversation turned to the damage done by the storm, the roofs to be repaired, the livestock that had needed rehousing till animal sheds could be repaired. Good tales were told, fine wines consumed, and, after a short period when the men were left to themselves, paying token homage to tradition, they regrouped in the drawing-room.

"I'd like a word, Poppy," Robin whispered, taking her elbow and leading her to a corner beside wall-to-ceiling bookshelves.

"Take your pick — there must be millions here."

"I'm being serious, wretched girl," he laughed despite himself. "Look, I'm not entirely happy about that knock our new friend has suffered. I'm arranging an X-ray for him tomorrow, but it might help restore his memory if you were to tell him exactly what

46

happened while you were with him."
Poppy fought back her horror at the
very thought. "It might jog his memory
and help him fill in the blanks."

"I'm not spending a minute longer
in that man's company than I have to!"
she told him heatedly.

"Oh, come on, love. Mother told
me the way of things, but I'm sure
something can be worked out about
the cottage. Have a little charity, eh?"

"I don't feel charitable towards Guy
Devereau!"

"Taking my name in vain, Poppy?"

She swung round, embarrassed.

"You shouldn't go sneaking up on
people!"

"Why don't you go and do your
host bit with Annabel, Robin?" Guy
suggested, restraining a smile.

"Thanks, pal. I hoped you'd draw
off some of the fire."

"I'm burning up," Guy laughed.

"I guess I'll have to lend you Poppy,
then."

He winked at her as he sauntered off.

"Are you and he an item?" asked Guy.

"No, we're not!" she snapped. "As I've already said."

"Good, then you won't mind Esther's suggestion that you drive me home. She was kind enough to pick me up, but we can hardly expect her to turn out again when we're such close neighbours, can we?"

It was the last thing Poppy wanted, but she could hardly refuse. She could try, though.

"Of course not, but I'm leaving now."

"That's fine by me — I feel extraordinarily tired."

They were soon in the hall taking their leave.

"Don't forget: supper with us on Saturday," Annabel reminded Guy. "I can drive over and pick you up."

"How awfully kind," he replied. "But you won't have to bother — I've arranged for a hired car to be delivered in the morning."

"You'll come too, won't you, Poppy?" enquired Madge, causing Annabel to scowl.

"I'd love to," Poppy replied sweetly.

"I'll pick you up — hardly worth getting your car out," said Guy, which brought further killing looks from Annabel.

"Please don't bother," she felt bound to say.

"I insist," he replied, urging her towards the door.

"How well do you know the Hall?" he asked as they headed past her cottage and up the lane to his new home.

"Pretty well — my parents both worked there, and they weren't the kind to leave me to my own devices during the holidays."

"Home from home, eh?"

She stopped her mini at the base of some steps leading to an ancient oak door flanked by lichen-covered stone portals.

"I wouldn't say that, but I know my

way around." "Like to advise me on a colour scheme for the drawing-room? You have an artist's eye, and I'm afraid my tastes run a little to the colonial."

She was surprised and delighted by the invitation: she had often viewed those dingy, duck-egg blue walls and faded brown velvet curtains with distaste, longing to wave a magic wand and create a light and tasteful background for the beautiful mahogany pieces in the room. He watched her face light up with pleasure at the prospect of realizing her dream, but then her eyes narrowed suspiciously.

"What's the catch?" she demanded.

"My dear Poppy," his tone was conciliatory but her nerves tingled with alarm when he lifted a finger and stroked it down her smooth cheek, ensnaring a strand of hair and pulling it free. "Why are you always so suspicious? No catch, I promise."

"No bailiffs?"

"Not without following the letter of the law," he smiled. "I'm no

Rachmann — wicked, landlord type, in case you didn't know," he explained.

"I'll think about it — I am trying to run a business, you know, and this is usually the busiest time of year.

Though sales in her local outlets were disappointingly low this year.

"So — delegate! Train someone."

That thought had already occurred to her, before the recent fall-off.

"Don't try and run my life for me!" she snapped.

"I wouldn't expect you to slap on the paint or whatever yourself — just supervise the workforce, once the basic plan has been decided."

She just couldn't resist it.

"All right — it's a deal."

"Excellent — nine o'clock Monday morning all right?"

"Fine," she agreed with a quick nonplussed shake of the head. "Can I have my hair back now?"

His answer was to wind it tighter. "Are you coming in for coffee?"

"No, I'm not." Heaven knew what

that might lead to, though she had a rough idea!

"How about one of those mind-blowing kisses, then?"

"Stop it, Guy," she protested weakly as his head came closer.

His lips touched hers, warm and firm. She was determined to resist, but as his lips stroked hers, her control started to snap, and she closed her eyes. His lips pressed briefly against hers, lifted away, and she was free. Her eyes snapped open to find him smiling at her with satisfaction.

"You're detestable, Guy Devereau, do you know that?" she declared but without much conviction.

He laughed properly then. "I love you, too, Poppy Winters."

He let himself out and closed the door smartly. She revved away, not staying long enough to see how Guy Devereau started up the steps and then paused halfway to stare back with a puzzled frown before continuing into the house.

3

SATURDAY evening at the manse was a convivial affair. Poppy found herself seated between Robin and the vicar — doubtless Annabel's arrangement, since she herself was positioned on the other side of Robin between him and Guy. Guy must have had similar thoughts from the knowing wink he gave her when they leaned forward at the same moment. She replied, having made sure no one else was looking, by sticking out her tongue, gratified to see his chest shake with silent laughter.

The other guests were the local vet, Derek, and his wife, Shirley, and a pair of computer scientists who, though only in their thirties, had bought a substantial new house on the edge of the village. They used it at week-ends but they planned to live there in their retirement or when their skills became defunct.

The vicar was at his most entertaining, while Guy managed to tell stories that appealed to their host's somewhat strange sense of humour but went completely over the head of Madge, if not of the other females present.

"Do you have any children?" Guy asked Tanya, who was sitting opposite him.

"Well," she turned slightly pink, placed a hand on her stomach and shot an enquiring look at Bob, her husband.

He laughed. "Go on, darling — you've as good as told them now."

"Well," she said again with surprising shyness, in contrast with her otherwise confident demeanour. "It hasn't been confirmed yet, but we're pretty sure I'm pregnant — about six weeks, in fact."

"Leave it another couple of weeks and then pop along to the surgery," Robin suggested.

"Won't that fettle up your career?" Guy wanted to know.

"Heavens, no. We shall have a nanny at first, and there's a super crèche for later on at the firm where we both work."

Poppy knew instinctively that Guy disapproved of this arrangement, but of what import to her were his opinions?

"I may be able to work from home on a terminal linked to the firm's main computer. We haven't explored all the possibilities yet."

"When are you due to whelp then?" asked Derek, the vet.

"Darling, Tanya's not a dog!" his wife, Shirley, scolded wryly.

"It's all right," Tanya laughed. "I suppose about the first week of June. We're thrilled, aren't we, darling?" Bob smiled his agreement. "We've been trying for a baby for ages."

Poppy wondered if the other women in the room suffered her own fleeting jealousy. Tanya suddenly seemed to have everything: a satisfying career, a secure home, no financial problems and, on top of that, a husband who loved her very much and his child growing inside her. Fulfilment, indeed. She couldn't see that happening to herself.

Robin nudged her elbow and she came out of her reverie to find Shirley speaking to her.

"Oh, sorry Shirley — I was miles away."

And Guy was peering at her oddly — she hoped she hadn't voiced her thoughts aloud.

"I said could I pop down in the morning and look at your new designs?"

"Of course you can. Come for coffee."

"Can I invite myself, too?" asked Tanya.

"Oh, do."

"That's a smart top you're wearing tonight — you didn't make that?"

It was of black silk laced with silver and stitched with black sequins, the fringing on the three-quarter sleeves matching the rows on the skirt. No low necks and bare shoulders tonight — she knew the draughty manse all too well!

Yes, I did," she told Tanya. "Silk's very warm."

She wished she hadn't added that the next moment when Annabel declared: "She means the manse is bloody cold."

"Darling!" chided Madge in hushed tones, while the vicar appeared to notice nothing amiss.

The high-ceilinged drawing-room was just as chilly as the dining-room, in spite of the huge fire roaring up the chimney, and a small radiator opposite. Annabel stuck to Guy like a leech, but Poppy was happy to circulate.

"Come over here, Poppy," said Robin quietly, drawing her away from a group that included their host, the vet and Tanya.

"Sure, what is it?"

"I don't like the look of Guy." She glanced across and noted with concern that he was indeed pallid beneath his tan. "I'm going to arrange for tests in the county hospital on Monday."

"Monday morning?" she enquired, remembering her planned meeting with Guy to discuss the decor of his drawing-room.

"No, the specialist holds his surgery in the afternoon."

She explained what they had planned for the morning.

"Have you talked to him yet about those missing hours?"

"Well, um, not really, no."

"Do try, and right now see if you can persuade him to go home."

Great! Annabel was going to love her for that! Fortunately, as she made her way over, Tanya and Bob were just saying good-night to their hosts and Derek was returning from taking a phone call to announce that old Farmer Brewer was having trouble with a breech-presentation calving so they, too, had to leave. Guy unfolded his length as she reached his side, and stood up. As he did so he swayed slightly and she automatically caught his arm.

"Are you all right?" she asked.

"I'm pretty all in, actually," he replied, his brow creased with pain.

Annabel was standing on his other side, pouting at the sight of Poppy's hand under Guy's elbow. She let it drop, having no desire to make Annabel jealous. The poor girl was very young and unsure of herself for a nineteen year old. She supposed, with parents like hers, that the girl stood little chance of knowing how to make the best of herself. Madge made no concession to fashion, wearing sacklike dresses and leaving her greying hair straight and slightly unkempt. Maybe she should take the girl in hand? No, somehow she didn't think Annabel would appreciate that.

"It's been a super evening, Annabel," she said now. "But everyone else is leaving," except Robin who was just accepting a large brandy from the vicar, "and Guy's got one of his splitting headaches."

"He didn't say anything," came the suspicious reply.

But surely he didn't have to? He was obviously in distress.

A few minutes later she was releasing her seatbelt and opening the passenger door of Guy's hired Jaguar, outside her cottage.

"See you in church?" she enquired, standing on the road and leaning inside the car.

"I guess so," he replied, with a smile — he had guessed she didn't want a repetition of last night.

"It's expected of you!"

"I wouldn't miss one of Desmond's sermons for the world! I bet they're quite something."

"You'd be surprised!"

"Shall I pick you up?"

"No, thank you. We don't want people to think we're an item, do we?"

He didn't answer — he didn't need to.

★ ★ ★

Little groups had gathered outside the picturesque village church, amicably chatting in the stiff October breeze. Poppy was talking to Esther and George when Guy joined them.

"As you said — I was surprised. He's a different man in the pulpit. All that talk of Christian charity — and loving thy neighbour!"

"Desmond's a very caring man under all that bluff," Esther informed him. "If you're in trouble, spiritual or temporal, he's a good man to turn to. He was once an army chaplain. He's very approachable, for a vicar."

"Yes, I suppose he would be. But I still wouldn't send my daughter along for advice!"

Esther and her husband turned to speak to someone else.

"Do you *have* a daughter?" Poppy taunted.

"Of course I damn well don't! I'm not married, and I've always been very careful in that respect!"

Poppy's blood ran cold as a new worry surfaced. No precautions had been taken by either of them that night. Surely fate wouldn't be so unkind — not her first time?

A team of builders and restorers were at the Hall when she arrived the following morning. They had been there some time, she gathered, discussing the basic structural work, so she and Guy were able to get down to the business of a colour scheme for the drawing-room, the first room to be decorated, straight away.

Guy let her decide without interference, endorsing everything — to her surprise. The walls were to be papered in a silk-finish covering several shades lighter than the peachy tone in the Aubusson carpet; this was to be cleaned to restore its brightness. All the stucco work was to be brilliant white.

"What about the ceiling medallions? Could they be restored?" Poppy enquired.

They had been painted over, but faint traces of shepherdesses and their loves could be seen through the paint, and she was sure there was a book of the original designs somewhere.

"That would be expensive," said one restorer doubtfully.

"How expensive?" asked Guy. A figure was named, astronomical to Poppy's ears. "Fine — whatever the lady decides."

Everything would be restored and refurbished just as Poppy had dreamed! The brown curtains were to be replaced by other velvet ones in a soft creamy beige to match that in the carpet, while peachy lampshades in pleated silk would adorn delicately-wrought wall candelabra, replacing dingy parchment. The huge settees and armchairs were to be reupholstered and covered in fabrics to tone with the rest of the furnishings.

"No buttoned leather?" enquired Guy.

"Definitely not! These seats are

wonderfully comfortable — well, they will be when they've been resprung. Keep the leather look for your study. Oh! I'm sorry, Guy, if you want leather . . . I mean it's your home, and . . . "

"Forget it, I was teasing. I told you I'd trust your judgement, didn't I?"

Soon the experts had gone and Poppy muttered something about leaving.

"Have some lunch first. It's the least I can offer you. I have a casserole simmering in the oven."

"You can cook?"

"I surely can. But don't tell Esther or Madge. This is one of Esther's."

And it was delicious.

"I never thought Percy Hugh had a lot of money to leave," Poppy commented between mouthfuls.

"Not a brass farthing!"

"Well then, how . . . "

"How am I going to pay for all this? I'm not exactly a pauper, Poppy. I had several thousand head of cattle to sell along with the ranch before I came over."

"*Two* inheritances! Aren't you the lucky one?"

"No!" His vehemence startled her. "My father was a gambler. He squandered his father's money. It was Mother's that paid for my education in England."

"So that's why you've no Aussie accent!"

"Mother never ceased to be the English gentlewoman. If I had but known I would one day own a small corner of England, I'd have been down to inspect it like a shot. Instead I slogged my guts out over there to build up the biggest ranch for thousands of miles, working alongside the men. That's the only way I know how to live — I can't imagine being a gentleman farmer, just sitting back and giving orders."

After lunch Poppy did leave. Later she heard his car go past and paused to say a silent prayer for him at the hospital. She worked all afternoon till it was getting dark but still hadn't heard Guy's car return. Perhaps he went by while she was on the phone; perhaps he had things to do, people to see before he returned. What was it to her? She put a record on loud, and tried not to strain over the noise for the roar of a Jaguar engine.

Her phone rang soon after six.

"Poppy?"

She mustn't sound too irrationally pleased that he was calling her.

"Hello, Guy. I didn't hear you get back." Damn! She hadn't meant to say that! "How did you get on?"

"They've decided to hang on to me for a couple of days," he informed her, his voice grim.

And he'd chosen to tell *her*!

"They did? Why?"

"Oh — tests, brain-scans: that sort of thing. Anyway, I obviously didn't come prepared. No shaving gear — nothing. And I wondered . . . "

"You want me to go and get it?"

"Perhaps you could borrow some from Robin . . . ?"

"Oh, I'll get yours, if you like."

"I locked up, dummy."

"Oh, don't worry — there's always a spare key in the second geranium pot along on the terrace."

"Wonderful! I suppose every burglar for miles around knows it, too!"

"Do you want your things, or not?"

"Yes," he growled. "Visiting's at seven."

The pips went and she didn't hang on to see if he fed in any more money. Seven — that didn't leave long.

She had a sketchy wash and put on some lipstick and mascara, then dressed in a chestnut brown sweater with a rust skirt. A matching shawl went over her shoulder, worn like a plaid. Low-heeled boots completed her outfit. Before leaving her cottage she gathered together some fruit, flowers from the garden — rich ruby, bronze and gold chrysanthemums and dahlias — and a tin of home-made biscuits: it was the best she could do without prior warning.

Guy was obviously a tidy, methodical man, so she had soon collected together the things he needed.

Poppy was just letting herself out of the Hall when a white Mercedes sports car shot into the drive. She paused on the steps and watched as a tall, immaculate blonde slid out, slinky as a cat in a slim-fitting suit of hyacinth blue that matched somewhat hard eyes. The basque of the jacket made the most of her slender waist. She had model girl proportions: boyish breasts, narrow hips, and long, long legs in high, spiky shoes. Her silvery-blonde hair was coiled into a neat chignon, adorned with a velvet bow, her make-up so perfect it could have been enamel.

Poppy hated her on sight!

"Is this the right place?" she enquired in a supercilious drawl, a scowl marring the perfection of her smooth, tanned skin. "I'm looking for Cranford Hall."

"This is Cranford Hall," Poppy conceded.

"Oh, good. Tell Guy I'm here, would you?"

Poppy's hackles rose. Who did the woman think she was?

"He's not here. Is he expecting you?"

"I have an open invitation," the blonde replied in her superior tone. "Who are you? And do you know where he is?"

Poppy would have liked to lie and say no. As the other woman came nearer she noticed fine lines around her eyes — she must be thirty — or more. She derived curious satisfaction from the fact.

"I'm a neighbour. Guy's in hospital," she reluctantly confessed.

"In hospital! My God! What's wrong with him?"

Poppy had an insane desire to giggle, but managed to keep a straight face. The mere thought of any permanent damage to Guy somehow wiped the smile off her face. "A tree fell on him — or rather on his car."

"Is he . . . ?"

The blonde looked more annoyed than distressed.

"He's just having a few tests — he has a memory lapse around the time of the accident. They want to find out if there's any permanent damage. He may never recover those lost moments, it seems."

"Really?" Hyacinth blue eyes slid away — there was something decidedly sly about her, Poppy decided. "Tell me what happened."

How could Poppy not? She told her what she knew of the accident — she had heard all about the crushed cab of the Range Rover by now — but omitted the fact that he'd spent the night at her cottage.

"So if he hadn't been there at that particular second . . . " The blonde looked thoughtful. She looked up, straight at Poppy. "If he hadn't stopped to phone me, he would have reached the

Hall all in one piece. How absolutely ghastly!"

She sounded like a bad actress, reading her lines all wrong.

"I'd better get along," said Poppy. "I don't want to miss visiting hours."

"Oh, you don't need to go. I can take those things."

"He asked me to go, and who knows what the shock of seeing someone else might do to him in his fragile condition?" she said with exaggerated concern.

"Y-yes, all right, then. I'll follow you."

They walked into the ward together. Guy's eyes settled on Poppy the minute she entered the room, her bright hair loose about her shoulders, her wide green eyes warm and caring as they sought his. He looked dark and vibrant against the stark white bedding, and strangely incongruous in stripey hospital pyjamas. It was only when they reached his bed that he noticed the other girl, who was

71

clearly put out. Poppy laid her armful of goodies on the end of the bed and while she did so the blonde hurled herself into Guy's arms.

"My poor darling! And to think it's all my fault!"

"What! Nerissa, what are you doing here?"

Poppy looked from one to the other. She could have sworn that Guy looked irritated, while Nerissa — silly name — was all false adoration.

"Darling, if I hadn't taken so long making my mind up you could have got off that phone and arrived safely at the Hall before that wretched tree fell!"

"What phone? What are you talking about, Nerissa?"

Nerissa laughed. "You can't have forgotten that, darling! You rang up to propose, and I . . . eventually accepted."

Poppy blanched. This woman was engaged to Guy!

"I — er — I didn't realize," Poppy

put in. "Look, if you'll excuse me, I'd better go. You'll have lots to talk about."

"You can't go straight back, Poppy." At last Guy addressed her. "Lovely flowers — from your garden?" She nodded. "Did you find everything?"

"I think so, and there's some fruit and biscuits in the tin there."

"Oh, how neighbourly," drawled Nerissa. "Darling, I can't wait to see inside the Hall. We'll soon smarten the place up — it looks a bit dreary at the moment. Thank God you look all right — I didn't know what to expect." She cast Poppy a deliberately reproachful glance. "When will you be out of here?"

"In a couple of days, I imagine."

"Oh, good! I'm staying with the Pemberton-Stuarts near Salisbury, so I'll pop down again when you're out — I hate hospitals!"

"I'm not that keen myself! Never mind, I expect Poppy will bring me whatever I need."

Which went down with Nerissa about as well as with Poppy herself.

"I think hospital visiting is more in Madge's line. Perhaps she'll bring Annabel."

"Darling, who are these people?"

"They're — oh, some of my new neighbours. How long did you stay in Australia?"

"Long enough! God, all that dust and flies! I spent six weeks there altogether. Still, just think, if I hadn't accepted my cousin's invitation, we'd never have met!"

"No," said Guy thoughtfully.

"I'm off," said Poppy, sick of playing gooseberry.

"Hang on to the spare key, then you can let the builders in, in case they want to make a start before I'm allowed home."

"Perhaps you'd like me to stay at the Hall, and tell them what to do," suggested Nerissa.

"No, I've already done that, and the drawing-room decor has already been decided. The decorators can make a start there."

"You've chosen a colour scheme?"

"Yes."

"Well, I'm sure if you've chosen it, I'll love it."

"I'm very happy with it. Poppy advised me — she has a wonderful way with colour."

"You mean . . . "

Narrowed blue eyes moved in hostile perusal over Poppy's pink face. She lifted her chin and glared back, then looked at Guy.

"I really have to go, Guy. Shall I ask a nurse to bring something for that pain?"

Her emerald eyes glittered wickedly over Nerissa's slender back, but when the other woman turned her gaze in puzzlement to meet eyes gone suddenly blank, she entirely missed the reciprocating sparkle in Guy's.

"Thanks, Poppy. You do that."

What Poppy actually did was dash hell for leather out of there, before

Nerissa could hurry after her and pour out all the venom and recriminations she could see the other woman storing up in what, Poppy was certain, was a very scheming head. She drove home in equal haste, blinking hard to dash away inexplicable tears. Was Guy really going to marry Nerissa? Had he, way down in the Antipodes, fallen in love with her, and invited her to marry him? Did Nerissa love Guy, as much as . . .

Yes, poor, foolish Poppy had fallen in love with her dashing, arrogant landlord, who saw no reason why he shouldn't bundle her from her lifelong home into some other, as yet undecided abode — anywhere so long as she didn't cause him inconvenience. Well, he could think again — Poppy wasn't giving up that easily!

4

FOR the rest of that day and all through the next, Poppy worked away till she had a pile of fronts and backs and sleeves of sweaters to be pressed and sewn into garments. She was still working late in the afternoon when she heard a car slew to a halt outside her gate. Heavy footsteps on her path were followed by a peremptory rap on her door.

Goodness, where's the fire?" she asked, opening it to be confronted by Guy Devereau's thunderous face.

"Where the hell were you today?" he demanded.

"Wh-what?" she asked, puzzled and astounded by his attitude. "Have I missed something? What are you talking about? When did they discharge you?"

"I had letters to post, and things I

needed from the shops . . . I discharged myself."

"You fool! And I'm not your personal skivvy, Guy Devereau! Get your damn fiancée to do your chores!"

"I don't want Nerissa . . . damn it, woman — I don't remember proposing to her." He brushed past her and sat down heavily on one of the kitchen chairs. "Tell me about that night, Poppy, I mean, from the moment I arrived here."

"Why?" she asked, knowing full well why — Robin had already spelt it out for her.

"Because I can't bear to have a gap in my memory. For pity's sake — can't you understand? Robin may have been joking but suppose there is something I can't bear to remember? Suppose I did propose to Nerissa, and immediately regretted it?"

"Is that likely?"

"I knew her in Australia."

"So I gathered. Did you know her well?"

"Not as well as she'd have liked, I fancy. She was only there for a holiday. She's witty and attractive, true, but I couldn't see any point in starting something destined for an abrupt ending."

"She might have decided to stay."

"No, she hated Australia. Nevertheless, I was tempted to have an affair with her — I don't, however, remember considering her as wife material."

"Why not?"

"I've always had this fanciful idea that I would one day meet and immediately recognize the woman who would be my wife — you know, eyes meeting across a crowded room, seeing my unborn children in her eyes — that sort of nonsense. What was my frame of mind when I drove down here, I wonder? What could have prompted me to stop en route phone up Nerissa and propose? When could I have done that?"

"Perhaps when you stopped to eat? I offered you food and you said you had eaten somewhere on the road. Do you remember where?"

"No, I don't, so you're probably right — that's when I must have called her."

"It was a foul night. Perhaps she reminded you of sunny Australia? Do you fancy a cup of tea?"

"Thanks," he accepted. "Did I talk about the journey at all?"

She set the kettle to boil. "No, not at all."

"What the devil am I going to do, if I don't remember?"

"You must remember how you felt about her in Australia. Were you pleased to see her at the hospital? Did you lie there missing her after she'd gone?"

She turned to face him when there was no answer. He was staring at her strangely.

"Do you want me to be honest, Poppy?"

"Y-yes," she said doubtfully.

"I find the prospect of cuddling

up on a chilly night to the slim perfection of Nerissa a whole lot less appealing right now than the warm, soft curvaceousness," he stood up and started towards her, "of a certain Poppy Winters," he finished, sliding his arms round her and pulling her against him.

She went warm all over but tried to hold herself rigid and not give in to the almost overwhelming urge to put her arms round his neck and mould her shape to his.

"Is that a fact?" Her voice was embarrassingly husky. He nodded gravely. "Well, I'm not in the market for acting as stand-in for your absent fiancée! Take your hands off me, Guy."

"You can help me, Poppy," he said softly, ignoring her request.

"How?"

"I felt nothing — nothing at all when Nerissa kissed me. Do you suppose that's because of my amnesia? I mean I really tried to kiss her meaningfully back, but nothing happened — no shooting stars, no violins playing. If I were to kiss you by way of an experiment, as it were, do you think the result would be the same? I'm getting desperate! I want to be certain this is a temporary state, and that when I marry Nerissa, everything will be quite normal."

How could he be so cruel, using her like that? Then it occurred to her that perhaps he was deadly serious. Perhaps he wanted to be sure he could feel nothing for any woman. He had been the one to pull away last time, when she had responded so passionately. How could she let him kiss her now, without giving away her feelings for him?

"Poppy?"

His head lowered slowly. She pressed her hands against his shoulders, intending to keep him at bay but he locked her against his body, one arm purposefully circling her waist, the other hand sliding up to anchor in her hair and tilt her face up to his.

"Poppy."

He breathed her name against her lips and claimed them with his own. Her hands stilled on his shoulders, arrested by the feel of his lips sliding against her own, warm and firm and wholly inviting. With a muffled cry she slid her arms round his neck, pressing herself closer. Or was he doing the pressing? They clung in urgent need, their kisses growing ever wilder. His hands moved possessively over her back, exploring its curves and indentations, pulling her even closer. His normal reactions were in no way diminished! She felt his warm fingers moving over the soft skin of her midriff. Her head fell back with a helpless little gasp, offering the slender column of her throat to his questing lips. He stilled and looked down at her, the pupils of his eyes large and black, circled by a narrow band of gold.

"I'm not sure what we've just proved," he told her hoarsely, not attempting to remove his hands.

Flushed with need and embarrassment she asked: "Can I have my body back now, please?"

For reply he slid his hands free and tugged her sweater into place, then took her hands from their resting-place round his neck and lowered them to her sides.

"I'd say, Poppy, that if I'm going to go ahead and marry Nerissa, then I'm going to need a lot of help from you in recovering my memory."

So long as it wasn't that kind of help! If she were to disclose what had really happened on that stormy night, if it were to jog his memory, he would also remember proposing to Nerissa and his feelings for the other woman — Poppy couldn't bear that.

"The kettle's boiling. I'll make that tea," she said.

★ ★ ★

For the next week there was much to-ing and fro-ing along the lane to the Hall. Workmen's vans, delivery vans, utilities they came and went. Poppy concentrated so hard on her work that her output went up by leaps and bounds. Her orders were completed — she was going to have to look for further outlets for her sweaters. Perhaps she should embark on a sales mission to London and aim for the big time.

Guy had stayed away and she wondered if he'd now recovered his memory and was too appalled by what had passed between them and too shamefaced to see her, or if he'd decided that the sort of help he had elicited on his last visit was too risky, considering her hopeless reaction.

★ ★ ★

As she weeded her vegetable patch one frosty Saturday morning at the end of October, she became aware of several sounds in the lane outside. From the direction of the village came the high-pitched buzz of a moped approaching up the lane, still out of sight round the bend outside her cottage. From the other direction came the distinct sound of a horse's hooves cantering carelessly down from the Hall. The next moment all hell was let loose. The moped skittered to a halt, to the dismayed cries of its rider. At the same time a horse whinneyed and the shrill tones of Nerissa cut the air:

"You stupid girl! Don't you realize this is a private road? What the devil are you doing speeding up the track like that?"

"I wasn't speeding," came the shocked and frightened tones of Annabel. "I couldn't see you for the bend."

Another horse cantered more slowly to join the group, coming to a halt.

"What the devil's going on here? Are you all right, Annabel?"

It was getting too interesting for Poppy to go on pretending to mind her own business. She sauntered over to the gate.

"Having a party?" she enquired with a smile, which was rapidly wiped away at the sight of Annabel's tearful demeanour and torn jeans. Ignoring the others she went out and righted the moped, helping Annabel to her feet. "Come in, love, we'll soon have you cleaned up."

They had barely reached her gate when Nerissa stormed into the fray once more.

"Well, darling, say something! That stupid girl came careering round the corner and almost unseated me. Surely this is a private road, isn't it?"

"Cool it, Nerissa. Can't you see the girl's hurt?"

He slid down from his huge black stallion and handed Nerissa the reins. The next moment he was at Annabel's other side, helping her into Poppy's warm kitchen.

"Just sit there," he ordered the frightened girl, skilfully unfastening her helmet and removing it. "Does anything hurt?"

"Only my leg." She indicated the torn jeans' area. "I caught it on the pedal. Apart from that, I'm all right, I think."

"You didn't bang your head?"

"I didn't fall right off — I just sort of crumpled in an undignified heap," she explained in a wobbly voice. "I was coming to see Poppy. What does she mean, it's a private road surely I can use it to visit Poppy, can't I?"

"Of course you can. Nerissa doesn't understand. How fast were you going?"

"How fast *do* those things go? Thirty-five maximum, downhill, with a good following wind!"

"Whereas your dear fiancée was galloping along the road as if the hounds of the Baskervilles were in hot pursuit!" put in Poppy.

"Don't exaggerate, Poppy!" Guy gave her a scathing look, before returning to Annabel. "I think I can leave you in my neighbour's capable hands — she might even patch your jeans for you!" Which brought him a scathing look from Poppy. "She's very good at tending the injured, anyhow. Now, I'd better get back to Nerissa."

What had he meant by that remark about her tending the injured? Had he recovered his memory?

"How go the experiments?" she couldn't help but ask quietly, halfway along her path. "Reacting nicely to Nerissa?"

"I seem to be avoiding that kind of experiment these days," he surprised and pleased her by answering, his eyes at the same time resting hungrily on her mouth.

"So you still can't remember?"

"Unfortunately — or perhaps fortunately — no." They had ceased walking altogether, and just stood there looking into each other's eyes. "I still have a feeling you hold the key to those lost hours, Poppy Winters." She coloured delicately. "By the way, I'm having a trio of cottages renovated behind the hall. Would you care to come and look at them?"

"I'm not a professional decorator."

But she was pleased he had asked her, just the same.

"That wasn't the reason. I thought you might like first pick of them for your new home."

She blanched, then the heat of anger rose to suffuse her face. "I'm not leaving here, Guy Devereau. I'll fight you in the courts if need be . . . "

His eyes narrowed. "You'd lose."

"That remains to be seen. Anyway, hadn't you better go and pacify Nerissa," she suggested sweetly.

"Bother Ne . . . "

He seized her shoulder but at that moment Nerissa's voice could be heard, loudly complaining. The next instant her head appeared above the wall.

"Come along, Guy. It's far too nice a morning to waste, and Midnight's getting restless."

"Coming, Nerissa."

His hand fell away but he kept his

eyes on Poppy's. "I'll be seeing you."

She stood there watching as he disappeared through the gate, aware of Nerissa's puzzled scowl, then turned back into the house.

"Why were you coming to see me, Annabel?" Poppy enquired as she cleaned up the younger girl's grazed knees.

"Two things, really. First of all, I'd like to order a sweater to go with a skirt I've just made . . . "

"You make your own clothes?"

"I sometimes design them, actually," Annabel replied modestly. "Which brings me to the second matter I wanted to ask you about."

"Which is?"

"Well, I suppose you had some kind of training for the work you do?"

"I did my stint at art college, if that's what you mean."

"That's precisely what I mean. Oh, don't think I have plans to set up in competition with you — as if I could, anyway.

"What, then?"

"Well, I decided to take a year off after my A-levels, to discover what I wanted to do. I rather fancy studying fashion design, but I haven't a clue how to get started. I was hoping you could help."

Poppy was only too delighted, and, by the time she had finished giving Annabel the benefit of her knowledge, they were well on the way to becoming friends.

5

"FORGIVE my curiosity, Poppy, but why have you brought two large suitcases with you to market?"

It was a mild, muggy Wednesday in mid-November, market day in their county town of Dorchester.

"I've got some orders to deliver to my retail outlets, Esther. All the shops are on High Street and South Street, so I can drop you off first, if you like. You don't need to hang around."

In fact, Poppy had brought with her, not only the sweaters shops had ordered, but a good many extra ones as well, that she was hoping to sell. She had just discovered that in future she would need to increase her income considerably.

"I don't mind waiting. I haven't got much shopping to do."

Poppy emerged from her last call, pale and disappointed.

"Are you all right, love?" asked Esther. "I thought you looked a bit peaky when you picked me up."

"I'm fine," she lied, "but I'm going to have to look for different outlets. The story's the same everywhere. Nothing's shifting, apparently. There's not much money about, and what there is is being spent on basics, not luxury goods, like original-design sweaters."

"Perhaps you should open a market-stall!" Esther laughed.

"That's not a bad idea."

The mere thought of standing out in the cold brought a return of the nausea she had suffered the last few mornings. She parked near the vast market site, where they went their separate ways after arranging to meet afterwards. Poppy paused beside one stall selling just sweaters. They were cheap, quite well made, but mostly acrylic.

"What can I interest you in then,

love?" asked the stall-holder, a young man in his late twenties. He was tall and fair, with a cheeky grin — not bad-looking apart from rather shifty eyes. "Cor, with that hair, you should be wearing green. Trust Dave Hadden to know what suits a lady."

"So they tell me — it's not one of my best colours, actually."

"How about a nice Arran-style sweater. Keep Jack Frost at bay — if you want to keep him at bay, that is."

"How do you go about getting a stall here?" she surprised him by asking.

"You don't look like no market-stall holder, though there's a group of ladies like yourself doing a roaring trade in leather goods. What kind of line are you in?"

"Sweaters, actually," she laughed.

"You've got a bit of a cheek, haven't you? Sizing up the opposition, all blatant like that?"

Poppy sighed.

"It was only a tentative idea. Mine

are original designs — I couldn't afford to sell them at these prices."

His eyes narrowed speculatively.

"Got any samples with you?"

"Well, there's this one," she said, opening her jacket to reveal the autumn leaf design, "and I've got a suit-case full in the car."

"Cor!" His eyes ran over her shapely form as he examined the sweater she wore. "Sweater's nice, too."

"It's the sweater you're supposed to be looking at," she told him tersely.

"It's very nice — maybe we could do a deal. I've always fancied going up-market."

"You mean you'd sell them for me? How about price?"

She told him what she charged the shops who bought them from her, and then added a percentage for their own profit.

"I couldn't give you anything like that, but I reckon I could take them off your hands, if we can agree on price."

She did want to sell them, didn't she? They haggled a bit while all the time she did sums to work out whether it was worthwhile dealing with him. She could, after all, spend the time going further afield to shops in Salisbury, Bournemouth, Exeter, or she could just beaver away producing bigger quantities, that Dave Hadden would be certain to buy. What should she do?

"Okay, I'll bring them along, and if you like them, you can have the first lot at your price," she agreed at last.

★ ★ ★

"Is he giving you a good price?" were Esther's first words, when Poppy told her what she had done.

They were lunching in the 'Horse with the Red Umbrella'. The café had once been a theatre, and the rather odd name had been the title of the last production staged there.

"Not bad in the circumstances,

I suppose. He wants to go up-market — at present he's selling mass-produced Arrans and Shetlands. He's not actually paying a lot, but it'll save me the hassle of marketing them myself."

"Is that what you want? You did once mention making a sales trip to London's West End."

"I know — I suppose I'm settling for the easy option."

"Any particular reason?"

"Oh, I don't know, I suppose I've been feeling a bit under the weather and can't-be-bothered-ish lately."

Like suffering from several days' morning sickness! There was little doubt about it, Poppy was almost certainly pregnant — her feelings on the matter swung from excitement to downright terror.

"Robin said you weren't your usual self when he took you to the cinema last week." Robin not infrequently took Poppy out when the two of them were at a loose end — purely as a friend.

"Perhaps you should see a doctor," Esther laughed.

"I saw one only last night — two, in fact! That was a marvellous dinner, Esther."

"Thanks. I think I might have enjoyed it a little better if Guy hadn't brought that Nerissa with him. She really is a pain. But seriously, love, you ought to have a word with George."

She glanced sideways at Poppy's pale face, pausing momentarily on the violet shadows beneath her eyes with a puzzled frown.

"Perhaps I will," Poppy agreed, having no intention of doing so for the time being. "Have you finished your shopping, Esther?"

"I've just got to call back at the chemist's and pick up some drugs we don't keep at our dispensary. How about you?"

"I've finished. Oh dear, I don't think I can eat that, after all."

They always finished lunch with one of the wicked cream confections the place was renowned for. Today, however, the very sight of all that thick cream oozing out of the flaky, melt-in-the-mouth pastry started her stomach churning.

"Poppy dear," Esther began on the way home. "Don't think me a busybody — you know how fond George and I are of you but I really do think you should see a doctor. Those violet shadows under your eyes — and you're very pale. You know you can always talk to me, Poppy."

Poppy turned three shades paler.

"You've guessed. I've only just realized myself. Is it that noticeable?"

"Not to the lay person — remember I'm a doctor's wife, and I've had children myself. Are you feeling generally fit?"

"Bursting with energy most of the time. I just suddenly slump. The same with food: some things turn me green — at other times I could eat a horse, or more likely a whole cucumber or a barrel of crisp apples."

"Quite normal, then!" Esther laughed.

Poppy had retrieved her shopping from Esther's car and was just setting off up her path when Esther called after her: "Don't forget — I'm on your side, love."

Poppy smiled, grateful for the proffered support.

"Thanks."

"Between you and me," she followed up in a loud stage whisper, "I think it's rather exciting!"

A strange thing to say, Poppy mused, but truth to tell, she was rather excited herself. She felt less pleased, as she surveyed the empty shelves, about the price Dave Hadden had paid for her sweaters, considering the time it would take to replenish her stock. Fortunately she had a few private commissions from people like Shirley and Tanya and, of course, Annabel, to keep her going. She would need a constant supply of those with two people to support.

That evening Poppy was about to sit down to a chicken casserole with lots of mushrooms when Robin steamed into her kitchen looking angrier than she had ever seen him. So angry, in fact, that she backed away across the kitchen.

"What the devil have you been telling my mother?" he demanded furiously.

"Wh-what do you mean?"

As far as she could remember it was Esther who had been doing all the telling, or guessing!

"She refuses to serve supper till I've come over here and sorted out 'this mess' with you! What the hell's she talking about?"

Poppy blanched. Esther *had* got the wrong end of the stick!

"It's nothing. Your mother jumped to some unfortunate conclusions, that's all."

"All! Anyone would think . . . " He stopped short, noticing for the first time her pale face, the deep shadows beneath her eyes. She might feel worse first thing in the morning, but it was in the evenings she actually looked her worst. "My God! She's right! Poppy, you *can't* be pregnant! I mean, who the devil . . . ?"

"Could possibly have found me that desirable?"

She said it with a grin, even though it hurt.

"No, of course not, silly."

Suddenly all of Poppy's bravado collapsed and her face crumpled. Robin pulled her into his arms, tucked her head under his chin, and stroked her back soothingly as one would a child. At last Poppy indulged in the luxury of a good cry.

"Want to tell me about it?" Robin asked when she was calmer.

"I can't, Robin."

"You realize Mother thinks it's mine?"

"Now I do, yes. Don't worry, I'll soon put her right."

"I half wish . . . "

"No, you don't, and who wants a half-hearted man? I hope you'll always be my friend, though, Robin."

"You bet."

"Now you trot off home while I ring Esther and reassure her."

"You do that — I'm ravenous! That casserole really smells good."

"Stay and have some, if you like."

"No, thanks all the same. I'd better go and make my peace with Mother."

* * *

The following Saturday morning Annabel dropped in. She had become a staunch friend since the accident and had taken to sounding Poppy out on matters of clothes and make-up. At this delicate stage in their friendship Poppy was careful not to criticize directly but by subtle suggestion she was able to help Annabel to create a subtler, more attractive image.

Today with smart new jeans Annabel was wearing a sapphire blue jacket that made the most of her eyes, over a white sweater that matched her woolly hat. On her feet she wore flat leather ankle-boots, a far cry from the spiky heels she usually sported.

"What do you think?" she demanded, pulling off her hat and shaking her dark hair about her shoulders. Gone was the heavy mass of wiry, back-combed frizz. Instead her hair had been layered and conditioned and blown into a mass of shiny, casual curls.

"Fantastic! It looks wonderful, Annabel! All I can say is: who's the lucky man?"

"You guessed! Well, that's partly why I came to see you. I mean I wouldn't want to tread on your toes, if you and he . . . "

Oh no! Poppy turned away. Please, not Guy! Poppy couldn't imagine Annabel and Guy together, and anyway, what about Nerissa?

"I've no claim on anyone, Annabel," Poppy said quietly.

"Oh, thank goodness." Annabel let out an audible sigh. "I couldn't believe it when Robin asked me to partner him to Lord Delmere's do next week-end. You're sure . . . "

Poppy laughed her relief. "Sure I'm sure. I'm really pleased for you, Annabel. Have a cup of coffee — it's freshly made. And tell me what you intend to wear to this do."

"I was rather hoping you'd advise me."

"Any thoughts on the matter yourself?" she asked, handing Annabel a steaming cup of coffee.

"I tried on a few things in Dorchester. Gauguin's boutique have got a wonderful selection of slinky numbers in fabulous jewel colours." Yes, Poppy steered well clear of Gauguin's party collection with her red hair! "And Madam Isabel's got some pretty nice things, too — if a little pricey. There's a stunning black and silver outfit — a strapless dress with a matching jacket; and then there's a midnight blue velvet one I rather liked . . . "

Poppy could just see Annabel in the latter with her lovely blue eyes.

"You could wear your sapphire drop earrings with it," she thought aloud.

Besides, black and silver sounded a bit ultra-sophisticated for Annabel.

"So I could. And to tell you the truth — I think Robin would prefer me in something dark and discreet. He came to see me that day I fell off my moped. I'd just cried all my make-up off — I felt positively naked, but Robin said that's when he saw what I was really like, and I guess he liked what he saw."

"I'll bet he did. You're a very pretty girl — no need to hide behind layers of paint."

"I'm beginning to realize I don't need quite so much, anyway. I'd better go. I promised to pick up some shopping for Mother. I'd better not let her down. They've been very long suffering, my poor adoptive parents . . . "

"I didn't know."

"I hardly think the Desmond-Madge genes would have thrown up something like me."

"You could be right," Poppy laughed.

Annabel grimaced. "No need to agree so readily! Anyway, I've decided to turn over a new leaf and act a little more mature. This," she patted her new hairstyle, "is all part of my new image."

She left Poppy in reflective mood. Last year Robin had escorted her to Lord Delmere's annual do. His parents had been there, so had Tess, Robin's sister, then engaged to Simon, Viscount Delmere. Against his father's wishes he had trained to be a doctor. He had finished his training now, and was married to Tess. It had been such fun, she would be sorry to miss it. Ah well, back to the knitting-machine.

By the end of the afternoon Poppy had added several sweater pieces to the pile waiting to be stitched up, among them her friends' orders. The others would have to be sold on Dave Hadden's market-stall. Daylight was fading. There was just time for a short walk before planning her lone supper and seeing what television had to offer.

Other young people, single and heart-free, would be getting ready for a night out at the cinema, or a restaurant, or maybe something more active like tenpin bowling, disco-dancing, or ice-skating. Sometimes she felt positively middle-aged. Sad too, because now she would never do any of those things. Poppy was not heart-free, she was carrying the child of the man she loved, which must remain her secret forever.

Donning warm jacket and wellington boots she strode off across the field opposite, with no particular destination in mind, but her footsteps carried her over the hill and up the lane to the three cottages that Guy was having renovated.

They were sturdy dwellings of traditional flint and brick, with a big gable over the extended front elevation and a small dormer window set in the sheltered section of the roof. They must be quite spacious inside. Was there any point in sticking out against Guy's wishes? After all, how could she bear to live close to the Hall, once Guy and Nerissa were married? She could always take cuttings of the plants she used for her dyes and grow them in the garden here.

From this angle, the Hall loomed large on the next rise, looking most imposing against the western horizon where the sun was sinking fast. A chill breeze started up. She had better start for home while she could still see her way in the increasing gloom.

Suddenly something pale and floppy appeared around the side of the cottages. She stared in surprise as a cream Labrador puppy, barely three months old, lolloped towards her, leaping up to lick her hand as it reached her.

"Hello," she laughed. "Whose guard dog are you?"

"Sheba! Down!" roared a familiar voice, its owner too emerging from the other side of the cottages.

"She's yours?" Poppy asked as Guy strolled towards her.

"She is. Creeping up in the dark to inspect your new abode?" he asked with a smile, which was not altogether unpleasant.

"No, I just felt like stretching my legs now I've finished work for the day." She looked away from the eyebrow raised in disbelief, and squatted to play with the puppy which had grown tired of sitting to command and had started to play with some drifting leaves.

"What a gorgeous creature you are," she said, scratching the puppy about her floppy ears.

The puppy promptly rolled over and waved four sturdy but muddy paws in the air.

"You've made a hit there," declared Guy. "Get up, you incorrigible, faithless hound," he ordered, gently nudging the dog with his booted foot.

The puppy did so and stood looking from one person to the other.

"Now that you're here, albeit accidentally," said Guy drily, "you might as well look inside."

Taking a key from his pocket he opened the door, flicked on a light and ordered the dog to sit while they looked round. To give him his due, Guy had had an excellent job done on the cottage. Both kitchen and bathroom were newly fitted, and all the rooms had been cleanly if impersonally decorated. There was even a small extension on this one that would make an excellent workroom. Even so, she was not going to let him think he had won.

"Very nice," she agreed as they emerged into the chilly evening air. She snuggled into the warm collar of her jacket. "I must get back now — it's almost dark."

The sun had left a bright pink afterglow in the west while a moon almost at its fullest peered over the eastern horizon.

"I'll see you home," said Guy.

"There's no need — I know the way

like the back of my hand."

"Even so, it would be unchivalrous of me to allow you to walk home alone, after detaining you — and Sheba could do with the exercise. Besides, there's something I want to ask you."

She looked at him expectantly but he merely cupped her elbow in one large hand and steered her homewards.

"How's the rag trade?" he asked as they walked along companionably, side by side.

Was that all he wanted to ask?

"Fine! I've found a local outlet, as a matter of fact."

And she found herself telling him about her deal with Dave Hadden.

"What about your plans to take the West End by storm? Was all that spiel at the Wilsons' for effect?"

"No, it wasn't!" she denied crossly. "I've changed my mind, that's all — a woman's prerogative, I believe."

"But why?"

Because I'm expecting your child, and I can't see motherhood combining with big business! — she could have stormed.

"I have my reasons," she replied obscurely.

"Which are?"

"I don't owe you an explanation," she flared.

"No more you do." He turned her to face him. "What's this Dave Hadden like?"

"Wh-what do you mean?"

"I mean is the interest purely professional?"

She thought of Hadden's smart-Alec approach to life, his casually rendered endearments, and could have laughed at Guy's insinuation. As it was, a tiny curl of amusement lifted her lips.

"I'm right, aren't I?"

Even if he were, which he wasn't, there was no call for him to be scowling like that! He jerked her against him when she failed to reply. Her head fell back, her eyes feasting on his shapely lips. She could not have said a word if she'd tried. His head lowered swiftly, his lips hard on hers and she responded hungrily. When he finally lifted his head and ended the kiss she would have liked to prolong indefinitely, there was a gleam of triumph in his eyes.

"Perhaps I was wrong, eh, Poppy? Unless you dispense kisses like that to all and sundry."

"Of course I damn well don't! You took me by surprise, that's all."

"I must remember that."

A whimpering sound came from the region of their feet. Guy laughed and bent to fondle the puppy.

"All right, Sheba, I can take a hint."

Straightening up he recaptured Poppy's elbow and they resumed their walk, the puppy scampering about their feet.

"How much is he paying?" Guy asked suddenly.

"How . . . who . . . what are you talking about?"

"Your market trader, of course! What's he paying for your sweaters?"

She'd quite forgotten Dave Hadden

and the sweaters, aware only of the lingering imprint of Guy's mouth on her own.

"What is this? The Spanish Inquisition?"

It was none of Guy's concern, but she told him anyway.

"You have to be joking! Designer sweaters fetch ten times that amount in London. He's taking you for a ride. What did you say his name was?"

When they reached the stile Guy produced a lead which he attached to Sheba's collar. He hooked it over a post and leapt over, then turned to help Poppy.

"I can manage," she told him impatiently.

"Sure you can," he replied, holding her by the waist and lifting her down to slide the length of his body and remain tucked against him. "You wouldn't deny a poor amnesiac his pleasure, would you?"

She glanced at him swiftly, paling, wondering if there could be a double meaning to his words. Had he remembered the pleasure she had 'given' him? No, there was no hidden meaning — she was just being ultra-sensitive. He released the puppy's lead whereupon Sheba slithered under the lowest bar of the stile into the lane.

"Oh yes, would you like to come to Lord Delmere's do on Saturday?"

Poppy felt a swift dart of pleasure, which she just as swiftly suppressed. "I don't go out with other people's fiancés," she told him primly.

"For heaven's sake! Nerissa's away, and I'm not suggesting a dirty week-end in Paris. All the neighbours will be there, and I gather Robin's taking Annabel. We'll just go as friends — we could go as a group."

They were halfway up the path to her door, she realized. What should she do?

"Do you want a cup of tea?" she asked, not wanting to decide quickly.

"Can't, I'm afraid. I've got to get Sheba home for her next feed. Puppies are like babies — they thrive on routine."

"Much you'd know about that," she flashed back, ignoring the stabbing misery in her heart. His child would never enjoy the same loving care from him as this puppy. "Still, I expect you're right."

"Say you'll come, Poppy."

"I can't."

"Can't or won't? Look, this poor dog's starving but I'm not leaving here till you agree to come with me on Saturday."

"Guy, please!"

He leaned against her door, a smug smile lighting his handsome features. Sheba began to whine, demonstrating her hunger.

"You leave me little choice, do you?" She knelt to play with the puppy. "Do you realize what a monster you've come to live with?" she asked.

"Sheba finds me a quite lovable monster," he retorted equably.

"A dog of very little brain," she quipped, restraining a smile.

6

LORD DELMERE'S party was usually the smartest of the festive season, getting things off to a good start. Poppy sorted through her wardrobe after leaving Guy and decided that the only suitable dress for the occasion was the one she had worn last year — and that would never do. There was nothing for it but to splurge on something new.

It was what she wanted to do, anyway. She had an unaccountable desire to appear at her very best — perhaps while she still possessed a waistline? She set off early the next day and scoured the shops in Dorchester. By mid-morning she had almost given up hope when she found the very thing. In an exclusive boutique tucked in one of the town's oldest buildings she found a dress of velvet and shot-silk taffeta in peacock shades of blue and green with a low, heart-shaped neckline and a full skirt that rustled as she walked. It had a period look about it that would be perfect in the party setting. She would have to wear her black and silver shoes — there was no way she could spend any more right now.

Guy arrived exactly on time just as she was spraying *Je Reviens* on every pulse spot she could reach. Her chestnut hair was dressed high with silver combs, leaving her slender neck bare but for a few tendrils of hair. With a surge of excitement she lifted her chin and went down to greet her escort.

She could not afterwards say who was the more stunned. From the expression on Guy's face she knew all the trouble had been worth it, while he had never looked more handsome. He was in formal evening attire, looking big and broad and virile in a black jacket, his Australian tan startling against the pristine white of his shirt. Even his dark curly hair had been tamed to neatness.

"All this for me?" he joked, his voice uncommonly husky.

"Do I look all right?" she asked — absurdly.

Hadn't a glance in the mirror just told her so, and why did her voice sound so ridiculously soft?

"You look fabulous," he declared, solemnly lifting her hand and pressing his lips to her soft white fingers with their pink-varnished nails. "Your carriage awaits, *madame*."

Lord Delmere's vast Georgian pile was surrounded by parkland, landscaped originally by Capability Brown. At the end of a drive slicing through acres of carefully tended gardens, the house glowed a welcome from dozens of lighted windows. Guy parked his Jaguar alongside Mercedes and Porsches, an occasional Rolls Royce and one ferocious-looking red Ferrari, together with more mundane and modest saloons.

"Oh good, the Wilsons are here," she commented as Guy helped her out of his car. "They've hired a locum specially so that both Robin and his father could come."

"That's nice for you," said Guy, his scowl belying his words.

"Why are you looking so cross? Don't you like the Wilsons?"

She knew from Esther that Guy often played golf with Robin.

"Just remember who your escort is," he growled, his hand pressed firmly to the small of her back as they crossed the circular drive to the main entrance.

"And that I'm merely standing in for Nerissa," she reminded him.

"Shall we forget about Nerissa for this evening?" he suggested calmly.

"Well, *I'll* certainly try to," she assured him.

He swung her round to face him and, right there in the middle of the drive with cars pulling up and disgorging occupants all about them, he hauled her against him, his fingers digging hard into her shoulders, and pressed his lips to hers.

A peal of laughter forced them apart and Poppy stared up at Guy, shaken and embarrassed.

"I should say I'm sorry, but it wouldn't be true," he said quietly, "but I didn't mean to embarrass you."

"Poppy Winters! So early in the evening! Aren't you going to introduce me?"

"Tess!" Poppy cried, delighted to see her childhood friend, framed in the doorway. "I'd no idea you were home! What a lovely surprise!"

"No time to phone, I'm afraid. We only arrived at tea-time. Remember Simon?"

"How could I forget the groom who could hardly stay awake for his own wedding! Oh sorry, this is our new neighbour: Guy Devereau."

"Oh!" Tess exclaimed, obviously surprised, but she recovered quickly. "How do you do? I've heard about you, of course, from the family."

"It's a pleasure to meet you, Tess.

If I'd been your bridegroom I think I might have stayed very much awake!"

"Not if you'd been on duty for ninety hours, nonstop! Simon was doing his housemanship at the time," Tess explained. "He perked up once we got to Rome."

"Ah! I stand corrected. Where do you practise now, Simon?"

Once inside the house and after greetings formalities were complete, Tess whisked Poppy off to the ladies' room for a gossip.

"I thought Guy was engaged!" she exclaimed at once, when they were alone in a downstairs cloakroom. "What gives? It was like *Gone with the Wind* out there!"

"I — er — I don't know what got into him. I'm just standing in for Nerissa. She's away at the moment, and Guy needed a partner for tonight's do."

"Pull the other one — it's got bells on. He's gorgeous! And you're obviously dotty about him . . ."

124

"Don't!" Poppy begged, her lips trembling.

"It's all right — no one else would notice, but we've been friends for ever, don't forget. What's this Nerissa like? Mother thinks she's ghastly!"

"She's incredibly beautiful — and she's ghastly!" Poppy agreed with a laugh. "He doesn't even remember proposing to her."

"So Mother said — she probably seized her chance and made it up."

"She wouldn't dare — surely? Come on, we'd better go."

"You're right, and I can't wait to see the new, improved Annabel. My crazy brother is talking about her as if he's just discovered her, and she's been there, large as life and twice as obvious for as long as I can remember!"

"I think you'll be pleasantly surprised."

Poppy didn't feel like a stand-in at all that evening. She was able to introduce Guy to many more of the locals, but they remained as a group with the Wilsons, sharing a large table for the delicious buffet supper which was served halfway through the evening.

Fortunately they sat some distance from the area reserved for smokers — Poppy had discovered that one whiff of cigarette smoke made her feel sick these days. She now discovered that wine had much the same effect, and set her glass down with a grimace. Esther leaned across her husband to speak to her.

"Would you like a Perrier?" she asked quietly.

"I'd love one."

"George, go and get one for her, love."

George looked curiously from one woman to the other and shrugged.

"Thought the wine was rather good, myself."

Behind his departing back they exchanged a conspiratorial giggle.

"Thanks, Esther."

After supper there was dancing in the vast, chandelier-lit ballroom.

"I think as your partner the first

dance is mine," said Guy, leaning towards Poppy.

She was only too happy to oblige, and allowed him to sweep her into his arms to move in time to the dreamy music.

"God, you feel wonderful," he told her, inclining his head to press his cheek to hers, and running his hand around the narrow indentation of her waist over the soft velvet of her dress. "Victorian glamour without the stays!"

"Do you have to hold me so tightly?" she asked feebly, melting into his solid length.

"Just shut up and dance," he ordered softly.

When the music had stopped and he led her back to their table she still felt in a dream. Tess's cheerful voice broke the spell.

"We're all going riding in the morning," she said brightly. "How about you two?"

Tess knew very well they weren't a 'two', but her choice of words had not ruffled Guy — why should Poppy be bothered?

"Count me in," said Guy. "Poppy? I can offer you a mount."

Oh God, did pregnant women go riding at this stage? She glanced at Esther in confusion.

"How can you refuse? Tanya and Derek are going and she's several weeks *pregnant*!"

"As you say: how can I refuse? And thanks for the offer of a mount, Guy."

"My pleasure."

She supposed it would be the fine bay Nerissa had been riding, but what did it matter?

"May I?" asked Robin as the music started up again. "How are you, love?" he asked as he steered her protectively round the floor.

"Blooming, I think the word is," she replied cheerfully. "Apart from that, I'm beginning to wilt, and I've got misgivings about getting up early to go riding. I'm not at my best first thing in the morning."

"I see, and it's difficult to get out of it without awkward questions being asked?"

"That's about the size of it."

"Of course, you might feel less sick if you were in a stable relationship, i.e. married. Like to tell me who did this to you?"

"No, I wouldn't, so stop digging."

"Look, if you really want to call it a day, the parents are off home soon. They'd give you a lift, rather than break up the party."

Glancing over at their group Poppy saw Guy in earnest conversation with Lord Delmere. Perhaps it would be best to make her excuses, and insist on Guy staying — after all, he was the one who had been invited.

Guy, however, saw things differently.

"You did what? You arranged this with Robin? What the hell's it to do with him? If you want to go home, *I* shall take you."

"But you could stay — you're just

getting to know everyone. I don't want to drag you away."

"What the devil's wrong with you? Are you coming down with flu or something?"

"Y-yes, that must be it," she agreed, only too happy to seize on his words.

"Well, why didn't you say so? Come on, say your good-byes and I'll get your wrap."

In the warmth of her kitchen he turned her to the light.

"You look pretty good to me," he mused. "Apart, perhaps, from slight shadows under your eyes. Women's problems, I suppose."

Poppy could have laughed if she weren't eating her heart out for him, so gloriously handsome in evening attire.

"Chauvinist pig," she managed to murmur.

They stared at each other for long moments, then his head lowered slowly to hers. Automatically she lifted her lips for his kiss, her eyes drifting closed. She felt his warm lips unexpectedly against her eyelids, first one, then the other. Startled, she raised her eyes to his, and caught her breath at the intensity in them. They fell to her lips and the next instant his lips were on hers, while his large hands found her waist and pulled her against him. He kissed her with a hunger that left her breathless and shaking when he finally pulled away.

"If I catch your flu will you come and nurse me?" he asked huskily.

"I haven't got flu," she returned, her voice equally soft.

"What, then? Did you just want to be alone with me?"

"Don't push your luck, Guy Devereau! I just wanted to go to bed — alone!"

"Spoilsport! Oh well, I'll call for you in," he consulted his elegant Rolex watch, "approximately seven hours' time."

"Really?" she groaned. "I don't think I can stand it."

"Being apart for so long?" he grinned. "I could always stay."

"Go away, Guy," she said, giving

him a gentle push. "Think of Nerissa."

"I thought we weren't going to think of Nerissa tonight?"

"You can hardly dismiss your fiancée to the point of bedding another woman!"

"If I could, I wonder what that would suggest," he said enigmatically. "Good-night, Poppy."

Why did he have to be so attractive, so amusing, so — lovable, she mused, as the Jaguar roared off up the lane? What was she to do? Soon it would be impossible to conceal her condition, from him or anyone else. Not everyone would be as understanding and supportive as the Wilsons. Should she move right away from the district? If she was going to have to leave the home she loved, why not leave completely and make a fresh start, somewhere where no one knew her? She could perhaps put about a story of widowhood, or something.

No, she was being ridiculous. This is where all her friends were, and it was not so very unusual for a single girl to have a baby these days. She fought down memories of the gossip that always circulated about such girls, the speculation, the hasty marriages. It was usually a nine days' wonder, and that was how it would be with her.

* * *

Poppy had set the alarm for half past six: an hour ago. Guy would be here any moment and, in spite of the weak tea and dry biscuit she had consumed on rising, and a refreshing shower, she still felt as sick as a dog.

"Oh no!" she groaned, hearing the clattering of hooves in the lane.

The next moment there was a sharp and disgustingly cheerful rap on her door. She would just brave it out and hope the fresh air of morning would drive the nausea away — or at least keep it at bay. Taking a deep breath she opened the door.

Guy stood there, brimming with

vitality and wearing an absurdly happy grin. It faded at once at the sight of her deathly pale face.

"Good God, what on earth's wrong with you, Poppy? You really are ill!"

"I'm okay," she assured him, looking beyond him to the two horses tied up at the gate. "It's just . . . "

Lack of sleep, she had been about to claim when a fresh wave of nausea hit her. She dashed through the house and up the stairs, only just making it in time to the bathroom. Afterwards she rinsed her mouth and splashed her face and turned round almost colliding with Guy.

"What are you doing up here?" she muttered angrily.

"Get that damned riding gear off and get back in bed," he ordered her. "I'll go and phone Robin."

"I'm all right," she protested. "Probably something I ate last night."

"Are you allergic to shellfish or something?"

"Y-yes, that's it. Of course!" she

agreed gratefully.

"You didn't actually have any," he gritted at her. "We ate the same, and I'm perfectly all right. Now get undressed, or I'll undress you myself."

The moment he disappeared down the stairs she threw off her jacket and jodhpurs and everything else and slid under the bedclothes. He was soon back.

"As I thought — no one else has been affected by last night's supper. I suggested that one of our eminent medical friends call to see you later."

"Thanks. You'd better hurry up, or you'll miss them."

"Miss . . . ? Oh, the riding! I'm not going — I decided that there was a little filly here in need of a bit of neighbourliness.

"Guy, I'm all right, really," she said, touched that he should be concerned. "And there was no need to call the doctor."

"No, Robin said it's all part of the same thing." Thanks for nothing,

Robin, she groaned inwardly. "There was a girl in the outback, working in the stables, with something like this," Guy was saying. "She even took to reading the same kind of books."

Poppy glanced up, startled, whereupon Guy took a book he had been holding behind his back and threw it on the bed: *The Stages of Pregnancy.*

"I — I expect Tanya left it," she improvised hastily.

Guy lowered himself to the bed and clamped his large tanned hands round her shoulders.

"Admit it, Poppy — you're pregnant."

She stared back with wounded eyes, making a little moan of agreement as her gaze faltered beneath his.

"Did Robin tell you?"

"No," he said gently. "Is it his, by any chance?"

"No, it isn't, but he does know about it — so does Esther."

"Anyone else?"

"Not yet — though I imagine that won't be the case much longer."

"Too right — there's no time to lose."

"For what? You don't think I'm getting rid of it, do you?"

He stared at her in surprise.

"Actually no, I didn't think that. I merely meant we must hurry up and get you married. Unless he's married already?"

"Stop trying to organize me, Guy! He's not married, but he doesn't realize he's about to become a father, and that's how it's going to stay. The thought of marrying me has never crossed his mind."

"You never struck me as a tramp." Her hand lifted and swept towards his handsome face but he was too quick — he caught her by the wrist and held it none too gently. "Or are you modern woman personified: exercising the right of motherhood without involvement?" he sneered. "Do you even know who the father is?"

"Yes, I bloody well do! Get out of here, Guy Devereau, and take your narrow, chauvinistic views with you! I don't ever want to set eyes on you again."

"That would be practically impossible, since we're neighbours." He actually managed to smile. "Sorry, Poppy, I just wanted to help — you're in one hell of a predicament. I'm going down to get you some breakfast and have a think — there must be some way out of this."

If only there were! He returned with a tray bearing fruit juice, toast and marmalade.

"Do you mind if I join you?" he asked. She noticed he had brought two of everything. "For breakfast, not in bed," he added with a smile.

"Be my guest, and thanks, Guy."

"I suppose *I* could marry you," he said absently.

"Mind you don't get stampeded in the crush," she joked.

"But seriously, if I don't recover my memory I shall marry Nerissa, without ever recalling the enthusiasm that led me to propose. She's a very suitable wife, of course, but I don't seem to react to her in a very . . . to be honest, in the way I react to you!"

"Forget it, Guy. I intend to marry for love, on both sides — the sort of marriage my parents had."

"You were lucky. That kind of love is rare. I certainly never knew it. My father was a drunken, gambling spendthrift. He sent my mother to an early grave. I swore my children would know what it was to have a father, someone playing an active role in their lives. That's why I don't want to think of your child, or any other, growing up without one."

"You can't marry every single parent, Guy, so thanks, but no thanks."

He couldn't remember proposing to Nerissa; he couldn't remember making love to her, Poppy. If he was ever cured of his amnesia, what exactly would he remember? Either way, she would be in the same dilemma, probably.

Two weeks after the Dorchester trip, she paid Dave Hadden another visit.

"Allo, darlin'," he greeted her. She winced inwardly at the false endearment. "You brought me another load? Sold like hotcakes, they did — not one left."

"Really? Well no, actually, I just came to see how they were going. Does that mean you want more?"

"As many as you can manage, darlin'. With Christmas not four weeks away, they make lovely presents. Tell you what — give me your address and I'll pop round and collect what you've got. 'Ow's that, then?"

Her instincts screamed against the idea, but why not? Sales were only picking up slowly in the shops. At least Dave Hadden would pay her on the spot — he had produced a roll of cash last time as if he always carried such money.

"All right then."

She gave him her address and he promised to call the following Monday.

★ ★ ★

On Sunday morning they were all gathered outside the church as usual after Desmonds's service.

"How are you, love?" Esther enquired.

"A bit better," Poppy assured her quietly.

"How are the sweaters selling? This must be a busy time for you."

"Busy, but I'm not getting much for them. Dave Hadden's sold out, apparently. He's coming round tomorrow morning for another batch."

Poppy had not heard Guy come up behind her but when Esther turned away he said: "Got his foot in the door, has he?"

"He's coming to buy some sweaters. Anyway, I wasn't talking to you."

"Where exactly did he sell the sweaters?"

"How should I know? These market

traders go to all the local markets: Salisbury on Tuesday, Wimborne on Friday, Blandford, Bridport — everywhere."

"You think he's on the level, then?"

"I suppose he must be."

★ ★ ★

She did not know how she expected Dave Hadden to arrive, but it certainly was not in the almost new Range Rover that drew up outside. She opened the door as he came up her path.

"'Ere we are then, darlin'," he said brightly. "Let's see what you've got now, shall we?"

"Cor, it's a nice little place you got 'ere," he commented, his eyes everywhere, missing nothing. "All yours, is it?"

"My parents', actually," some instinct forced her to reply.

"I see. They about?"

"No."

He picked up an ornament, turning

142

it over to examine the base. She had not intended to prolong his visit by offering him something to drink, but while she went upstairs to fetch down the sweaters, at least it might keep him in one place. She would have had them downstairs already had he not arrived early.

"I've just boiled the kettle. Would you like a cup of coffee?"

"That'd be very nice — Poppy, isn't it? Very nice, indeed."

Instant was quickest, and she was back in no time offering it to him and suggesting he sat down.

"I won't be a moment — I'll just get the sweaters."

She opened the door to the stairs.

"I'll come and help you down with them," he said cheerfully, putting his cup down and starting after her.

"You'll do no such thing!" came the icy tones of Guy Devereau. "Miss Winters is quite capable of carrying a few sweaters."

"Who the heck are you?" asked Dave

Hadden with a scowl. "You don't look old enough to be her father."

Poppy cast Guy a beseeching glance.

"A friend and neighbour," he replied coolly.

"I get the picture."

"I doubt it."

Poppy could still hear them snarling at each other as she bundled up the sweaters and carted them down the stairs.

"Here you are, then."

"Very nice. How many are there?"

He counted them carefully, then peeled some notes off a fat roll.

"You have to be joking! They're worth four times that much. That's daylight robbery!" Guy shouted angrily.

"Look, what's it to you, mister. The lady and I made a deal. She's 'appy, I'm 'appy. You 'er partner or somethin'?"

"No, but I don't like to see a friend cheated."

"I can't charge the earth on a market-stall."

"Where did you sell the last lot?"

"'Ere and there — Bridport, Salisbury. Mainly Salisbury — that's where the money is."

"You'd better not be cheating this girl — or you'll have me to contend with. Understand?"

"Sure thing. I'd better be on my way."

"I'll see you out," said Poppy.

"I was going to ask you out for a drink," he said in an undertone, halfway along the path. "I don't suppose his nibs would like that, eh?"

"I don't drink," she replied primly.

"Ah well, you can't win 'em all. I'll be in touch."

7

"**Y**OU'RE out of your mind to work for so little!" Guy exploded as she re-entered her kitchen.

"I don't see what it's got to do with you."

"You're going to need every penny you can get from now on. What is this Hadden to you, anyway?" he demanded, as if she had not spoken.

"What do you mean? What is he? What do you think? You surely don't think he and I . . . you seem to imagine I'm having an affair with every man I speak to."

"I don't know what to think any more. I came to ask you a favour, actually."

"What kind of favour?"

"I wondered if you'd look after Sheba for a few days — I have to go away."

146

With Nerissa, she wanted to ask, but of course, it was no concern of hers, even if it was. The woman had a perfect right to spend time with her fiancé.

"I'd love to," she replied.

"We're flying to Paris on Thursday, and should be home on Monday."

"Great," she replied dully, in no doubt as to the 'we'.

"Thanks, Poppy. Can I bring her down on Wednesday afternoon?"

"That's fine by me. What do I feed her on?"

She'll come complete with bed, food and instructions," he told her. "I'll see you then."

There was nothing for it but to work. Work, work, work. As soon as the place was tided up Poppy's day began. She may not be getting much for her work, but there was no limit to the number of sweaters Dave Hadden would buy.

Guy appeared as promised on Wednesday afternoon.

You're not to spoil her," he instructed.

"Her diet's written out, and she's not allowed on beds or furniture."

"We can go for walks, presumably."

"Of course — she's had her jabs. Not long walks, though — just a couple of miles while she's so young."

Poppy knelt to run her hands through the puppy's silky coat.

"You and I are going to have a lovely time, aren't we?" she said, fondling her, and receiving little whimpers of pleasure in return.

"Lucky Sheba! If I lay down like that, would I get the same treatment?"

"I'd be more likely to put the boot in!" she replied shortly, knowing it was not true.

She must be the world's biggest mug, looking after his dog while the man she loved went off for a romantic week-end with another woman, albeit his fiancée. He had gone quiet and she glanced up to find him regarding her rather oddly. He leaned over and pulled her to her feet.

"Look after her, and take care of

yourself," he said gruffly, his hands about her shoulders. "And think about what I said about getting married. The father has a right to know you're expecting his child, you know, and a duty to support it — and you."

"Thanks for your concern," she replied, as lightly as she was able. "And don't worry about Sheba — she and I will get along fine."

"I am grateful to you, Poppy. She's rather young to go into kennels, and, as you know, I don't as yet have any staff."

"For which you need the cottage! You don't have to keep reminding me. In fact, I rather fancy moving to one of those other cottages. You've had a good job done on them. The one with the extension would suit me very well."

"You do surprise me! I thought you were quite adamant about staying here, where you grew up."

"Well, I've changed my mind!" she snapped.

She couldn't bear to live so close to the Hall once he and Nerissa were married, and likely to pass her cottage several times a day. No, she would prefer to be tucked away over the hill, with a different route to the village.

"Thanks again," he said.

Before she could guess his intention his lips had found hers. a shock of desire skittered through her system, drowning out rational thought and she clung to him, kissing him back. When he drew away he looked as dazed as she felt.

"I'm sure pregnant ladies aren't supposed to get so excited," he murmured with a shaky smile. "I'd better try and remember where my obligations lie."

After he had gone, she wondered whether he meant in general, or if he was referring back to his amnesia.

Sheba certainly took her mind off thoughts of Guy and Nerissa, living it up in Paris. Her days revolved around feeding, grooming, walking and playing with the puppy. When she settled down to work, having exhausted Sheba for a while, the dog would rest her head on Poppy's feet, as if making sure she didn't escape while she slept. When it was time for bed, she would whimper pleadingly, glancing at the door to the stairs where Poppy was about to disappear, but Poppy did not give in. She had promised not to spoil the creature and, tempting as it was, she kept her promise.

The nights were difficult, however. Poppy often went down in the early hours to make a cup of tea and then she would stroke the sleepy puppy and speak soothingly to her. Upstairs she would lie in bed, trying to blot out pictures of Guy's tanned body entwined with Nerissa's slender form. Nerissa would be used to the sophisticated venues to which — Guy would take her; she would know how to please a man, too. When they returned, Poppy had no doubt they would have set a date for their wedding.

Were it not for loving Guy, those would have been delightful days. Perhaps she would get a puppy for her baby, but not right away. Let him get through his first year. Let him learn to walk first.

Him. She was quite certain it would be a him. Why, she didn't know. She just imagined he would be a small replica of his father. Handsome, demanding, and, later on, funny and adorable, and a male chauvinist, to boot.

Oh baby, I love you, she murmured, pausing in her work to clutch her stomach and rock gently back and forth in her chair.

Monday came and went. Halfway through Tuesday morning, she heard a sharp rap on the back door. Sheba sat up and made a great effort to growl.

"That's no way to greet your owner," she laughed, still smiling as she opened the door.

Her smile died. On her doorstep stood Nerissa, and by her side a middle-aged couple, the man of decidedly rough appearance, the woman of waxen complexion and with a wracking cough.

"I've brought the Lomaxes to look at the cottage," Nerissa informed her. "For goodness sake, don't let that dog jump up at me."

Nerissa was wearing an immaculate suede suit with a silky blouse and knee-high, polished boots.

"I wasn't expecting anyone. Guy didn't say . . . "

"Guy doesn't have to!" snapped Nerissa.

"He does, actually. Anyway, I haven't quite made up my mind." How dare he! She had only a few days ago mentioned that she was considering moving, and he sent his ghastly fiancée along with a most unlikely-looking couple. "Still, I suppose as you're here," she told the couple as politely as she could manage — after all, it wasn't their fault they were caught up in her domestic arrangements, "you're welcome to look round."

The woman's eyes lit up when she

saw the cosy sitting-room with its ingle-nook fireplace, comfortable three-piece suite and polished tables. She stretched her hands to the flames, sniffing loudly, and then giving an enormous sneeze. Poppy handed her a tissue.

"Furnished, is it?"

"No, actually, it's not." Poppy frowned. "Didn't Mr Devereau tell you? I mean, surely the advert . . . "

"Twas us that advertised," the man informed her.

He looked incapable of smiling, and was not the cleanest person she had ever met.

"For what, exactly?" she felt bound to ask.

"Really, I don't think that's any of your concern," Nerissa broke in.

The Lomax woman, however, sensing the animosity between the two of them, and perhaps feeling a little guilty about turning up on Poppy's doorstep without any advance warning, had other ideas.

"We had problems paying the mortgage," she informed Poppy, gaining a furious scowl from her husband. "We needed somewhere quick, so we advertised for a job with accommodation. Reg does a bit of gardening, like, and with three teenage boys, I'm not a bad cook."

Oh God, it was worse than she thought. When she remembered the sheer professionalism her father had brought to his work, the superb dishes her mother used to cook . . .

"It's quite small," she said gently. "You say you have three teenage boys. Do come and look."

She led them up the stairs to show them the two bedrooms. The woman's face fell.

"You're right, dear. It is rather small," she agreed. "Still, we'll manage."

"Course we shall," her husband, Reg, added sharply. "And I noticed an extension off the kitchen — that could always make an extra bedroom."

"There you are, then," said Nerissa triumphantly from the stairs. "I'll talk to Mr Devereau when he gets back."

"You mean Guy didn't send you?" Poppy enquired, smelling a rat.

"He had things to do in London. He thinks I've gone home, but I thought I'd surprise him. He'll be so pleased to have the domestic problem sorted out."

He would, if it was sorted out, but instinct told Poppy the Lomaxes weren't at all right for the post. For one thing, with three sons, Mrs Lomax would hardly be able to cook an evening meal and clear away afterwards. She'd have far too much to do at home.

"I wouldn't get too excited," she felt obliged to tell the couple. "I expect Mr Devereau will have other people to interview."

Which earned her a look of disappointment from Mrs Lomax and one of fury from Nerissa.

"There's a lot of work to do in the grounds," she told Reg Lomax. "I expect there'll be other staff, but as head gardener, you'd have to supervise them.

"I dare say," he replied tersely.

"I'm sure Mr Lomax will soon get the place up to scratch," Nerissa said patronizingly. "We'll have that rather bleak drive lined with shrubs."

"That's right!" agreed Mr Lomax defensively. "A nice edging of rhododendrons all the way from the gate — all colours."

"Any maybe a bed of azaleas in front of the house?" Poppy enquired in astonishment.

"Why not?" he growled.

Mainly because this was chalk land — rhododendrons and azaleas positively hated it!

She did not even bother to reply, changing the subject quickly, relieved when they finally went back outside. Sheba trailed after her along the path, staying close.

"Got a few weeds here," remarked Reg Lomax, eyeing her prize herb patch with distaste. "They'll have to go. I'll probably grass the lot over, or maybe keep a few chickens on it."

Horror compounding horror. Just go, the lot of you, she prayed.

"I'll be in touch, then," Nerissa told them as they reached the gate, turning back herself.

"Oh, I expect you want to take Sheba with you," said Poppy, surprised by how dismayed she felt at the prospect of losing her companion.

"I most certainly don't! I'm going to cook a nice little *dîner à deux* for when Guy gets home this evening. I don't want that wretched dog around." She smiled, like a cat. "We'll be able to carry on from where we left off in Paris."

"Did you have a good time?" Poppy felt obliged to ask, though she did not want to know.

"Fabulous!" Nerissa assured her. "A five-star hotel, dinner at the Ritz," — Poppy herself would have preferred a dimly-lit bistro — "dancing to the early hours in a *boîte de nuit* . . . And, of course, we had to pay a visit to Cartier's . . . "

Lifting her elegant left hand she gazed triumphantly down at the enormous solitaire sitting on her third finger. Poppy felt sick. She would kill the woman if she didn't go soon.

"I've never cared for diamonds myself," she found herself saying. "I find them rather cold."

"But you know what they say — about them being a girl's best friend!"

"Oh, you mean when the magic fades," she retorted with surprising venom.

There were more lines than she had at first noticed around Nerissa's cool blue eyes. She was probably in her mid-thirties, far too old for Guy!

"That will hardly happen to us, if Paris was anything to go by," Nerissa told here smugly.

"I don't think you should be telling me this," Poppy said.

She certainly didn't want to hear it.

"You're right. I just want you to get it straight — the sooner you move away from here, the better for all of us. Guy won't want you hanging around after we're married."

"And when will that be?"

"The first week in January," came the confident reply.

"I see. Oh goodness, it's time to feed Sheba. Guy is most meticulous about punctual feeding times, as you'll no doubt find out."

"I shall certainly not be the one to feed it," Nerissa replied, and, turning on her heel, she left.

"Oh, Sheba, I hope you didn't understand that," she told the puppy when they were back inside.

She knelt and fondled her and, in return, Sheba put her head on Poppy's raised knee and looked soulfully up at her.

"I don't think you're going to like Nerissa any more than I do," she said.

★ ★ ★

Guy turned up at ten o'clock the following morning, looking terrible.

"Heavy night?" Poppy offered in mock sympathy.

"Bloody awful," he snapped. "Why didn't you let Nerissa bring Sheba back while she was here?"

"Mainly because she refused to take her! And don't come in here shouting at me. Why aren't you over the moon? Nerissa obviously is! A week-end in Paris, a ring from Cartier's, last night's romantic *dîner à deux*. I suppose she's still in bed this morning."

"You know, Poppy, you're beginning to sound like a jealous woman. Paris was Nerissa's idea, and I believe it's normal to buy a ring for one's fiancée. I arrived too late and too tired for dinner last night." He frowned. "How did you know about all that?"

"I got it from the horse's mouth, chapter and verse," she informed him tersely.

"Is that a fact?" She could have sworn his mouth quirked in amusement — could it possibly be for her likening

Nerissa to a horse? "Anyway, Nerissa's not best pleased with me at the moment. She's taken off — not that it's any of your business! And she tells me you did your darnedest to put off some couple who wanted to work for me!"

"They weren't suitable!"

"Who the hell are you to say who's suitable, and who's not?"

"I know the Hall, and its grounds, Guy," she said quietly. "I felt rather sorry for the woman, but with three teenage sons this place would be too small anyway, and she wouldn't have had the time to act as housekeeper . . . "

"Nerissa said nothing about three sons. I thought it was just the two of them."

"And he didn't know the first thing about gardening. He planned to plant rhododendrons all the way up the drive, and a bed of azaleas near the house."

Suddenly Guy's shoulders began to shake and he laughed aloud.

"Now I wonder how you found that out?" he murmured.

Poppy gave him a wary look then she, too, started to laugh.

"I was pretty furious with Nerissa for turning up without a word of warning, actually," she confessed.

"Did she?" he murmured absently. "And how has Sheba been?"

He went down on his haunches beside the dog-basket, rubbing the puppy's ears. She squirmed contentedly and went back to sleep.

"I've really enjoyed having her, Guy."

"She looks reluctant to move."

"Come on, Sheba. Your master's home," she said brightly, going down beside Guy.

A rumbling sigh was the only response. Poppy looked at Guy, a smile on her lips. He was staring back. Her smile died and suddenly they were in each other's arms, still half kneeling on the floor. The kiss went on and on, ceasing only when

Sheba bestirred herself and tried to join in.

"I think you're a witch, woman, you know that? One look at you and I get all kinds of wicked ideas, whereas in . . . "

He brought himself up short. What had he been about to say? In Paris? Hadn't things been as perfect as Nerissa had made out?

"Nerissa loves her ring," she said inconsequentially.

"Yes, it rather suits her, don't you think?"

She did, but was it for the same reasons as Guy?

"It does."

"Now diamonds wouldn't suit you at all. You should wear something like emeralds, or rubies, or maybe yellow diamonds. Yes, yellow diamonds would suit you very well, I think."

"Oh, do stop theorizing, Guy. Are you going to take Sheba now, or not?"

"Come on, Sheba. I know where

I'm not wanted, and now you've spoilt my fun, you can come along home with me."

Fun! Was that what she was to him? Just a little light diversion from the main game, from Nerissa, soon to be Mrs Guy Devereau. Oh, how could she bear it?

Guy hitched Sheba's leash to her collar.

"I'll collect the rest of her things in the car," he said, pausing in the doorway. "When's Hadden due to call next?"

"Any day now, I shouldn't wonder. I haven't actually done much work — we've been too busy having fun, haven't we, Sheba?" She bent to say her farewell to the puppy. "Now, don't you let him bully you, will you?"

Later that day a huge bouquet arrived beautiful yellow roses. She looked at the card. *All my love*, said the bold, spiky letters. No name? She turned the card over. *From Sheba, with thanks*, she read, a burst of hysterical laughter rising in her throat. Ah well, the next best thing to yellow diamonds from a lover of one night — yellow roses from his dog!

8

DAVE HADDEN called a few days later, on the first Monday of December. Why had Guy been interested in when the man called? If Poppy had had Dave's telephone number she would have called him and told him not to bother. Not only had she had less time to work, with Sheba to look after, but she had also had less inclination, now she suspected he was severely underpaying her.

To cap it all, she had woken up the previous day with a fiendish headache and the beginnings of a sore throat — probably caught from poor Mrs Lomax. Today she felt much worse and was certain she was running a temperature. The pile of fronts, backs, and sleeves remained, as yesterday, unsewn.

"Morning, darlin' — 'ow are we

this morning?" Dave Hadden greeted her cheerfully later that morning. He frowned when he saw her pale face with just two spots of livid colour on her cheeks. "Oh dear! Not feeling so chirpy, eh?"

"I feel terrible," she replied, her voice coming out all husky, but not in the least sexy. "I'm afraid you've had a wasted journey."

"You must have something for me!"

"Only half a dozen — hardly worth your bothering."

"I'll take them — 'elp you out a bit. I'll call next week when you're feeling better. Just you get a nice big pile ready for me — I promise to take all you've got. I'll probably be able to get rid of them before Christmas."

When he had gone she looked at the pitifully small cheque in her hand. She couldn't live for a week on what was left once she had replaced the wool. When she felt better she would go round her retail shops again. When she felt better she would also look for

168

new outlets. But for now . . .

She made some lemon and honey and slowly crawled back upstairs and into bed. Later on she would make a fire, but right now, she hadn't the strength to refill the hod for the Aga . . .

She heard her name through a fog of pain. Hammers seemed to be pounding her brain. Every muscle ached; her throat felt tight. She shuddered violently and started to cough. Why was the room so cold? And why did her chest hurt so much when she coughed?

"Poppy," said a deep voice. "Why didn't you tell me you were ill?"

"Guy? What are you doing here?" she managed. "How . . . ?"

"Don't talk, love. If you're wondering how I got in, I figured if the Hall had a spare key under a geranium pot, there might be a similar arrangement here. I had to search around to find the one loose stone in the crazy paving. Just stay there. I'll go and make you a cup of tea and call Robin — or George."

It was George who called, George who shooed Guy out of the room and examined her, taking her raised temperature, listening to her wheezy chest, feeling her lumpy glands.

"Is it flu?" she asked croakily.

"Can I come in?" asked an impatient Guy from the landing.

"You can," George called back. "It's a bad dose of flu," he told them both, "and a touch of pneumonia, I'm afraid."

"Oh, no!"

Poppy's face crumpled. People like her didn't get pneumonia, did they? How on earth was she going to cope? What would she live on while she felt like this, unable to work?

"Don't cry," Guy soothed, sitting down beside her and taking her in his arms. "What's the treatment then, George?"

"Rest, plenty to drink. Don't worry — this type of pneumonia's not the disaster it used to be. I'll drop some tablets in later today."

"Can't I collect them?"

"Certainly." George's pleasant face, an older version of Robin's, betrayed his inner doubts. "Actually, I think I'd better see if they've got a bed in the local hospital. Poppy needs to be properly taken care of. Esther would have done it like a shot, but unfortunately she's staying with Tess for a few days. I gather she and Simon have also gone down with this wretched flu — it's quite a potent strain this year."

"She can come to the Hall — I'll look after her."

"You, Guy?"

George regarded him curiously. He knew, of course, of Poppy's condition. He also knew that Guy had spent a night here at the crucial time. Could he be her child's father? If so, why didn't she say so?

"I shan't be alone — I interviewed a couple yesterday who will suit me eminently. They'll be moving into one of the renovated cottages shortly, but they were free to start work immediately, so they'll be living in at the Hall for a few days while we get their furniture installed."

"Well, that seems a sound arrangement. What are they like, this couple?"

"They're in their late forties. Ken's been Lord Ravenwell's assistant head gardener for a few years, and fancied a post where he could move up a rung or two, and be in charge. Dora's been running a pastry shop-cum-café. They're cheerful, hard-working — couldn't be better, really."

"Excellent! The sooner Poppy's out of here, the better. The place is like a morgue. I think the Aga's gone out."

"I got that impression, too."

Soon they had both gone, the doctor to attend his other patients, Guy to fetch the tablets and make sure a room was ready for her at the Hall, but not before he had filled a couple of hot-water bottles for her. Poppy had drifted back to sleep by the time he let himself quietly back in. He packed a few essentials and carried her, wrapped in a blanket, to his car.

He carried her out the other end, too, taking her straight into Cranford Hall and up the stairs. When he lowered her into a deliciously warm bed she clung to his neck, reluctant to let him go.

"Thank you, Guy," she said in her maddeningly husky voice and to her horror, tears pricked her eyes and rolled down her cheeks.

"Just returning a favour," he told her, unclasping her hands and tucking them under the covers.

The days passed in a haze of doctors' visits from both George and Robin, feverish sweats, violent shivering attacks, all interspersed with the cool, soothing hands and warm, velvety voice of Guy. He was always there when she needed him, day or night, with drinks, medicine, pain-killers, but mainly the reassurance of his warm, vital presence.

There was also Dora Knight to offer light but nourishing food, cheerfully changing her sweat-drenched sheets or sponging her down to keep her comfortable. Ken, her husband, looked in once to say hello and bring her a bunch of flowers from the overgrown garden.

"You won't know the place by next summer," he told her. "Mr Devereau wants it restored to what it was a few years ago, when your father had the care of it. There's a lot of work to be done, but the results will be worth it. Just you wait and see."

Only she probably wouldn't be here to see it. Once Nerissa was installed, Poppy would hardly be a welcome visitor.

At last she passed the crisis point and her temperature returned to normal. She just felt washed out and weak as a kitten.

"I've brought you a visitor," said Guy one afternoon.

Sheba waddled delightedly across the room her front paws going up on the bed so that Poppy could fondle her.

"My, you've grown! How long have I been here?"

"Just over a week," Guy informed her. "No, Sheba, you certainly can't get on the bed."

Sheba went to lay obediently on the floor at the foot of the bed.

"You've been very kind, Guy, but now I'd better be getting home," said Poppy, not wanting to go at all.

"Don't be absurd! You're in no fit state to look after yourself. You can stay a few more days at least, while you get back the use of your legs."

"Will Nerissa mind?"

She had not seen anything of Nerissa, but she must surely have been here. People who were engaged would want to spend every possible minute together, wouldn't they?

"Nerissa's enjoying a mad social whirl in London, right now," he said somewhat grimly, probably quite cross to be deprived of her company. "She'll doubtless be down in time for Christmas."

Guy, on the other hand, had been here every day and every night. He must be missing Nerissa dreadfully.

He did not have to wait for Christmas. The very next morning, while he was out discussing the kitchen garden with Ken Knight, and Poppy was contemplating getting up and taking a bath, Nerissa breezed into the room. She stopped dead when she caught sight of Poppy.

"Well!" Her hands went to her narrow hips. "You didn't waste any time while my back was turned, did you?"

Poppy was shocked to silence by Nerissa's accusation. Fortunately at that moment, Dora Knight, after knocking timidly, entered the room.

"And who in the name of heaven are you?" Nerissa demanded rudely.

"I might well ask the same of you," Dora replied calmly.

"I'm Guy Devereau's fiancée," came the proud retort. "And I'd like to know what this woman's doing in my room!"

Nerissa's room! That meant she didn't share Guy's bed when she stayed — not every night, at any rate.

"Poppy's been very ill, and she's here at Mr Devereau's invitation. I'm his new housekeeper, so I take my orders from him," she stated pointedly. "He wants Poppy to be kept warm and quiet, till she's recovered."

Bully for you, Dora! thought Poppy, grateful for her loyalty.

"Does he, indeed? Well, I'll just take the things I came for and have a word with him on the matter. What happened to the Lomaxes, by the way?" she asked Poppy.

"Guy wanted a professional gardener, who knew better than to try and grow rhododendrons and azaleas on chalk!"

Nerissa's eyes narrowed and, without another word, she swept out.

"Oh dear," said Dora, quietly closing the door. "I hope Mr Devereau won't be cross."

"Why should he be? She wasn't very

nice to you. And thank you for coming up I don't think I could have coped with her by myself. You'll probably get used to each other, once they're married," she added forlornly.

Dora observed her expression.

"I'd have credited him with more sense. Never mind, there's many a slip 'twixt cup and lip. Shall I run you a bath now, dear?"

"Thank you, Dora. I think I'll get dressed today."

"That's more like it."

Guy had only packed a few things for her, among them a lilac sweater and toning skirt. When she put them on, they hung loosely on her, and she was able to see just how much weight she had lost. There was an undeniable swelling at the base of her stomach, however — evidence that the baby at least was doing nicely.

After rubbing her hair dry she applied some light make-up and proceeded downstairs, where she found Guy in his library, his back to the fire, his gaze somewhere in the middle distance.

"Poppy!" he exclaimed, pleasure evident on his face.

"Where's Nerissa?" she asked tentatively, accepting his supporting arm gratefully as he led her to an armchair near the fire.

"Nerissa couldn't stay," he informed her equably. "I hope she didn't say anything to upset you — she can be tactless. She's still enjoying pre-Christmas London."

"Shouldn't you be enjoying it with her?"

"Country life suits me fine," he said a trifle grimly. "She didn't upset you, did she?"

Poppy was surprised at his concern. Shouldn't he be more interested in how Nerissa felt?

"No, of course not. She was quite surprised to see me, I suppose," she said carefully.

"Mm," he murmured thoughtfully. "How about a game of chess this afternoon? Or would you just like to have a quiet read?"

"I'd love a game of chess, but I mustn't keep you from your work."

"You won't be. I've been working all morning, and the phone is just through there," he indicated a door leading off the library, "should it ring. I've rigged up an office in there. Come and see."

She accepted his helping hand as she stood up but then her legs, weak from lack of use, gave way and she stumbled. He caught her at once, holding her firmly against him.

"Strewth!" he exclaimed, revealing all those years in Australia. "You're all skin and bone, girl!"

"Thank you, kind sir."

She knew it was true, but she couldn't prevent tears of helplessness from pouring down her face.

"Sorry, Poppy, but you have lost weight. All those nice rounded curves gone — well, most of them. "With a grin, he produced a pristine white handkerchief and proceeded to wipe away her tears. "We'll have to fatten you up."

"Like the Christmas turkey! I'll be putting on weight soon enough," she reminded him.

"So you will," he said bleakly, his eyes leaving hers. "Come and take a look at my office."

With one arm firmly round her slender waist he led her through to a very functional office with a desk, filing cabinets, a large computer, its colour monitor flickering away, and a fax machine.

"I can run my businesses from London to Australia from right here," he told her.

"You still have interests in Australia?"

"Some investments in the finance sector, and a holding in a high technology company," he informed her.

"Impressive!"

"Which is what I've been concerned with this morning, after sorting out a few problems in the kitchen garden, and why I think I deserve a little diversion this afternoon."

"All right, you're on. Chess it shall be, but I really must go home soon."

"You're in no fit state to look after yourself. Give it a few days."

"I could get used to being spoilt," she laughed.

After less than an hour her concentration began to wander; she stifled a yawn. "That's enough for now," Guy decided firmly, wheeling the table away, the chessman still in place. "I'll see how lunch is coming along."

She spent that afternoon and those that followed in the library. They sometimes played chess or Poppy would read while Guy did likewise, or made some calls in the adjoining office.

"I must go home tomorrow, Guy," she told him regretfully one afternoon. "I have work to do: sweaters to sew up and others to make."

"All good things come to an end," he joked.

Had it been good for him? She had loved being a part of his household, and would miss him dreadfully when she was back home.

"You've been so good to me, Guy. I don't know quite what I would have done without you."

"You'd have gone into hospital, or managed down there, with some district nurse popping in on her rounds. I was just being neighbourly. Out in Aussieland, we had to take care of each other."

He was standing in his favourite position in front of the fire. She looked up at him from her armchair. He was so handsome, so vibrantly healthy — yet so kind. Their eyes locked. Right now, his expression was not exactly one of kindness, more one of hungry, masculine need.

"Guy?"

He took her hand and jerked her up and into his arms.

"Oh, Poppy, I don't know what you do to me. The place won't be at all the same without you."

He held her as if she were made of porcelain. Slowly his head lowered till their lips met. The force of her response shook them both. Her too thin body, cradling his child, moulded itself to his, while his responded in kind. When he put her away from him, for she could not draw away, his breathing was ragged.

"Back to normal," he commented with a grin. "You're leaving not a moment too soon."

A gentle tap presaged the arrival of Dora, who walked in to find them standing there, their arms still loosely about each other.

"Lunch is ready, sir," she announced, and Poppy caught the housekeeper's satisfied smile as she turned to go.

"Dora approves of you," Guy told her.

"She doesn't know I'm pregnant," she replied.

"I do, but it doesn't seem to make you any less fanciable."

"You've been alone too long."

"Mmm," he agreed absently. "Let's go and eat. I'm starving."

★ ★ ★

"When's that Hadden character calling again?" Guy enquired while they were having coffee.

Lunch had been a tasty, filling stew, rich with vegetables Poppy could almost feel the pounds creeping back on.

"He usually calls on Monday mornings. He's probably been round while I've been up here, in fact. I'd better get to work right away."

"I want a word with him when he comes. I'll look out for him."

"Oh Guy, I can cope with him."

"I'm sure you can, love, but there's no reason why you should."

And there was no reason why Guy should use superfluous endearments, as he had taken to doing of late.

★ ★ ★

Once Poppy was home, however, she was disinclined to make sweaters for Dave Hadden. For one thing, she had little energy, for another, everyone who called, it seemed, from Esther to the vicar's wife, Madge, including Tanya and Shirley, wanted to make sure she was all right and, at the same time, give her business a boost. They all ordered sweaters for themselves for the cold months ahead, and others to give as Christmas presents.

She set to with a will, happier to work in the knowledge that she would be receiving a fair price, enabling her to pay the mounting bills.

Annabel was one of her first visitors.

"I'm starting the art foundation course after Christmas," she told Poppy delightedly.

"That's great news!"

"Yes, they're letting me start a term late. They liked my portfolio, and my enthusiasm, it seems. Why don't I stitch some of these up for you?" she asked, viewing the pile of knitted pieces on the table.

"To tell you the truth, I could do with some help. I've suddenly got loads of orders, and the sewing up is the part I like least! I could pay you a reasonable hourly sum."

She mentioned a figure.

"I don't want to be paid — I thought I might learn a few trade secrets, about design and generally running a fashion business. Not that I'm aiming to compete — I want to design glamorous evening dresses and bridal wear, and maybe children's clothes."

"You are going to be busy! Seriously, though, I couldn't accept your help without paying you. It'll be hourly, while the work lasts."

"All right, then. You're on."

The two girls worked well together and if Annabel wondered about Guy's ongoing concern for his recently sick neighbour, she never questioned his almost daily visits.

9

AT the week-end, Tess called on Poppy out of the blue.

"Simon and I are spending the week-end here. We're expected at his home for Christmas, so we're having an early celebration with my parents. Can you come for lunch tomorrow?"

"Thanks, I'd love to."

"Guy's coming." She paused. "Poppy, why didn't you tell me?"

"About what?" Poppy asked guardedly.

"Well, about the baby, of course! It must be due about the same time as ours. Sorry, but my stupid brother let it slip — some doctor! And why are you coping alone? He is the father, isn't he?"

"No, your mother jumped to that . . ."

"Not Robin — Guy! The way you two look at each other — it just has to be!"

"Oh, Tess, you don't understand."

"Try me! For heaven's sake, we grew up together. What are friends for?"

And Poppy found herself pouring it all out to her old friend. It was such a relief to confide in someone she could trust completely.

"I can see it's a bit tricky, but, from what you say, he himself thinks the father has a right to know, and a duty to support the baby."

"But if he doesn't remember . . . and if he does recover his memory, he'll also remember proposing to Nerissa, in which case whatever feelings he had for her will be rekindled — either way, I shall still be out in the cold, and he'd have one hell of a guilty conscience to live with. I can't do that do him, Tess. I . . ."

"Yes? You were saying?"

"You know what I was trying to say: I love him too much to burden him with that."

"Oh God, you're hopeless. Guy's man enough to decide for himself,

189

but he must have all the facts first! See you for lunch, eh?"

Was Tess right? Should Poppy tell Guy precisely what had happened on that wild and stormy night, and let him decide what to do himself — what part, if any, he wanted to play in the life of his child?

Perhaps she should — and soon. The first week of January, when he and Nerissa were to be married, was less than a month away. Nerissa would be furious, of course, to start married life knowing he shared a permanent link with Poppy in the form of a child.

Supposing he claimed the child though, she suddenly thought in terror? Supposing he decided that he and Nerissa had more to offer a child than she, Poppy herself? They did, in the material sense, of course, but Poppy loved this child already, and she was quite sure Nerissa would be nothing but a cold and heartless mother, even to her own children — let alone someone else's.

That Saturday night she barely slept a wink, tossing arguments over and over in her mind. By morning, she decided that Tess was right. Guy must know, and make his own decisions. She would tell him after lunch with the Wilsons. She would ask him to call on his way home, and then she would tell him.

★ ★ ★

In church on Sunday morning, Tess made a warning face at Poppy and rolled her eyes towards the pews at the front of the church. These were set at an angle to the other pews, and had traditionally belonged to the Devereau family. There, beside Guy, in a tailored purple suit, over which she wore a short fur jacket, was Nerissa. Her blue eyes wandered in Poppy's direction, gave a little triumphant smirk and returned to Guy, whom she favoured with a brilliant smile.

The corner of his mouth barely lifted,

but his eyes were drawn to Poppy. Her small smile was acknowledged with a solemn nod. His eyes remained on her, however, taking in her still-pale face and lean cheek-bones. Her slender body was hidden beneath a practical, tartan-lined duffel coat.

Nerissa's sharp eyes followed the exchange and brought it to an end by the expedient of sliding her hand over Guy's. She had removed her gloves, and the magnificent diamond sparkled in the light of electric lamps switched on to dispel the winter gloom.

Poppy joined in anthems, carols and responses like an automaton, saying her own little prayer in between for some answer to her dilemma. After the service she stayed talking to friends for as long as was polite, studiously avoiding Guy and Nerissa, and turned away to her car.

"How are you?" asked a familiar voice just behind her.

"Getting better all the time, thanks, Guy," she assured him, swallowing a sudden lump in her throat.

"That's good." She glanced round at the unexpected bleakness of his tone. "See you at the Wilsons."

"Yes, see you there."

★ ★ ★

Despite the general conviviality around the lunch table, Poppy felt tense and alone. There was no chance now of talking to Guy, either here or afterwards when they left for their respective homes. Nerissa took every opportunity to stake her claim to Guy, blithely talking of their plans for the Hall once they were married.

"I'm afraid we shall have to go now," she told Esther who had only just served coffee. "Guy's coming up to London with me this afternoon. We've been inundated with invitations: Guy's really been missing out!"

"I also have a few business matters to attend to," Guy reminded her soberly.

"I expect I can spare you occasionally,

but we've got a lot to catch up on," she told him with a fulsome smile.

"How long will you be away, Guy?" Tess asked.

"A couple of days, I expect."

"A week, at least," Nerissa insisted.

"I do have work to do," Guy reminded her kindly.

"Don't be stuffy, darling — it's nearly Christmas."

"Which is why I must get things done before the business world shuts down for two weeks."

"I expect Simon and I will be gone before you get back, in any case," Tess told him, "but we'll be back for a few days around New Year."

"Excellent! I was thinking of throwing a Hogmanay party on New Year's Eve. I hope you'll all come — it's time I returned some hospitality."

There were general murmurs of assent and acceptance and Guy left, almost reluctantly, it seemed, with Nerissa.

"Come and see the new skirt I

bought," Tess invited Poppy. "I'm hoping to persuade you to make a sweater to go with it."

"I'll give you a hand in a minute with the dishes, Esther," Poppy called back as she followed her friend from the room.

"No problem — the menfolk love stacking the dish-washer. They have an ongoing contest to see who can pack the most in!" Esther laughed.

"Have you really bought a new skirt?" Poppy asked as she followed Tess up the wide staircase to her old room which she now shared with Simon.

"Yes, I have, but, as you've guessed, I wanted a chat. It's a pity they had to dash away. In fact, it's a pity Nerissa's in the picture at all — do you get the impression, as I do, that all's not well with those two?"

"I put it down to wishful thinking. You can't get round the fact that Nerissa's the one with Guy's ring on her finger, the one who's going to marry him shortly. I don't somehow think she'll relinquish that position lightly."

"She'd make him desperately miserable! She's a townee, who just likes to play at country pursuits from time to time, whereas Guy loves it down here. He likes dogs and I bet he's marvellous with children. He wants to put down roots take my word for it. I guess I just felt like giving you a bit of encouragement — you looked so down in the mouth over lunch."

"Thanks," Poppy returned drily. "And I thought I was being bright and cheerful."

"You were — overbright! And I wasn't the only one to notice it."

"Who else — not Guy?"

"The very same! He's concerned about you, I can tell. Where are you having the baby, by the way?"

"I haven't thought that far ahead."

"I'm coming down here so that Mother can look after me. I think it's marvellous that they're due about the same time they'll have a ready-made friend in each other."

And they chatted on about their coming state of motherhood, though their circumstances were so different. Poppy began to realize that there were many practicalities she had not yet considered. Her life was about to change for good with the arrival of this baby.

★ ★ ★

By Wednesday Guy was back at the Hall. Poppy saw nothing of him but she heard his car once or twice, and noticed the lights blazing away after dark. Was he alone? Or was Nerissa with him, she wondered?

Annabel had already left the following afternoon when Guy walked in. Poppy was feeling rather pleased with herself as she packed the last of the finished sweaters, beautifully stitched up by Annabel, into its cellophane wrapper. Work was the one thing that kept her mind from constant thoughts of the man who had just arrived. She viewed the scowl on his face with some dismay.

"How've you been?" he asked tersely, as if he had been away for years, and not just the four days since they had last seen each other.

He slumped onto one of the kitchen chairs, resting an arm on the well scrubbed surface of the table.

"I've been fine, Guy — and extremely busy. Annabel's a tremendous help. We're right up to date with orders. How about you? Been living it up in London?"

She had tried to sound flippant, but failed abysmally. He certainly looked as if he had hardly slept since they had last met, and she would rather not go into the reason why.

"No," he snapped moodily. "I've been working bloody hard! Both in London, and since my return! Any chance of a cup of coffee?"

"Of course. I was about to have

some myself." She filled the coffee-machine and switched it on, aware all the time of Guy's eyes following her every movement. "How's Sheba?"

"She's fine — I don't think she missed me, either." Either? "As long as someone feeds her and walks her, she doesn't give a damn who it is!"

"Oh dear, we are grumpy today," she said with a smile, audaciously patting his cheek.

The next moment she wished she hadn't. In a flash he had seized her wrist and hauled her onto his knee.

"Did *you* miss me, Poppy?" he demanded, his voice suddenly hoarse.

Miss him! She had spent every moment she was not actually working, and often even then, thinking of him, what he was doing, how he was feeling.

"I've been busy working, Guy," she told him quietly, her gaze unable to meet his. "And, anyway, what right would I have to miss you? You're engaged! Is Nerissa at the Hall now?"

"No — I left her in London."

"You prefer to work down here?"

"I prefer to *be* down here — don't you realize that?"

"Th-the coffee's ready, Guy."

"To hell with the coffee — this is what I need."

Refusing to take no for an answer he seized her chin and angled her lips to meet his. She mustn't respond, she wouldn't — yet she did. In no time at all, she relaxed against him and slid her arms round his neck.

"Oh, Poppy, what am I going to do about you?" he asked huskily.

"Right now, you're going to have a cup of coffee," she told him, taking advantage of his relaxed state to escape from his embrace. "And you can tell me how Ken Knight's getting on in the garden."

She set down two cups of coffee and deliberately sat opposite him, with the table firmly between them.

"The man's crazy about the walled kitchen garden, and he has no plans for azaleas and the like, you'll be glad to know. But I didn't come here to talk about vegetables. How's the cottage industry? Has Hadden been round?"

"No, which means he'll call next Monday, I suppose. I rather wish I hadn't dealt with him in the first place."

"You don't have to deal with him now, if you don't want to. I'll see him for you."

"Why on earth should you?"

"I want to, Poppy. I want to help you. Here you are, a girl living alone, trying to run a business, and also expecting a child without the benefit of a husband. You seem to bring out the protective instinct in me. I want to help you."

"And Nerissa?"

"I'm sure a wife would understand my motivation."

And Poppy was equally sure she wouldn't — any more than she would understand their recent warm embrace!

"It's not right you should be coping

alone," he went on. "Are you sure you wouldn't like to tell me who the father is? I'm sure we could get this all sorted out, without too much trouble."

Now was her chance. Should she tell him? She had intended to last weekend, but then he had taken off with Nerissa. She gazed into his amazing light hazel eyes, now full of concern for her, not as the object of his love though he did seem to fancy her — but as another human being who had made a mess of her life.

"Oh, Guy," she began, the words trembling on her tongue.

A light, staccato rap sounded on the door. For a moment they just sat there, staring at each other — a frozen tableau, teetering on the brink of something important.

"You'd better see who that is," Guy suggested resignedly, reacting more quickly than Poppy.

She stood up and took the few steps to the door, her eyes widening in dismay and horror when she saw

202

Nerissa standing there.

"Is my fiancé here, by any chance?" she asked superciliously.

"Er, yes, he is, as a matter of fact. Come in."

"Oh, how cosy!" she exclaimed, looking round as if referring to the kitchen, but Poppy knew she meant the two of them sitting there, like some married couple.

"Darling, I just couldn't stay away," she told Guy effusively.

"What about that reception you were going to this evening, and tomorrow night's cocktail party?"

"Unimportant!" she declared airily, with a dismissive wave of the hand. "I decided I'd much rather be with you, at Cranford Hall. After all, it'll soon by my home, too, so the sooner I get used to it, the better."

Guy stood up, scraping his chair back as he did so.

"We'd better get back there, right now," he said, ushering her out through the door, an arm round her shoulders.

"Thanks for the coffee, Poppy."

The words were an afterthought. Poppy watched incredulously as they went up the path together, Guy's arm round Nerissa's shoulders.

"We have to talk," she heard him say as they reached the gate.

She closed the door and leaned against it with a sigh. Nerissa had decided which side her bread was buttered, and renounced her social engagements for Guy. Had she found it difficult to do so? For Poppy, there would have been no real choice. Her love for Guy would have won, hands down.

They had now gone back to their future matrimonial home together, to make plans for the future — plans which in no way would include Poppy.

To think she had almost told him about the baby. She could never tell him now. Nerissa only had to show her beautiful face, and Poppy ceased to exist. There was no way she could now unburden herself to him, and risk losing her child to him and that woman. Nor did she want to create difficulties for him — she loved him too much.

★ ★ ★

That same evening she was washing up after supper when she heard a noise. Pausing in her task she listened carefully. There it was again, a whimpering somewhere close by.

Taking her sturdy rubber torch she opened the back door. The sound was clearer now, coming from somewhere near the gate. She went up the path and shone her torch into the lane. There, cowering in a miserable heap, was Sheba, muddied and dirty, her large ears hanging dejectedly.

"Sheba!" Poppy cried, opening the gate and walking towards the puppy. "What on earth are you doing here? Guy will be mad with worry."

The puppy wriggled towards Poppy, looking up sheepishly, as if downright ashamed. She needed little encouragement to bounce up and give Poppy a friendly lick on the face, however.

"You'd better come inside. I'll let them know where you are."

It was not Guy who answered the phone, nor even Nerissa, but the cheerful Dora Knight.

"Hello, Poppy. Are you feeling better, my dear?"

"Much, thank you, Dora. I phoned because I've got Sheba here . . . "

"Sheba? But she was with . . . I'll let Mr Devereau know. Thanks for ringing."

Suddenly, it seemed, Dora couldn't wait to get off the phone. Was she suddenly *persona non grata* with everyone at the Hall? She had hardly had time to give Sheba a drink and clean up her coat when she heard the Range Rover outside.

"Here's your master," she said. "He'll be glad to have you back. Come along."

She opened the door at the sound

of heavy footsteps on the path. It wasn't Guy, however, but Ken Knight, walking up her path.

"Here's the little truant," Poppy said cheerfully, ushering Sheba out.

She walked towards Ken, wagging her tail.

"He'll be right glad to have her back," he said, fondling the puppy. "I don't think any of us realized she was missing. Thanks for looking after her, Poppy. You feeling better now?"

"Heaps better, thanks."

"I'll get her back. Times we all want to run out, but it won't do," he told Sheba darkly, leaving Poppy wondering what he meant.

On whom would Ken ever want to run out? Surely not Dora — a nicer person no man could have for a wife. Guy, perhaps, in one of his darker moods?

What business was it of hers, anyway? She returned to the sink to finish the dishes, empty with disappointment.

Whatever she may have decided to

do, or not to do, she realized she was acutely disappointed that it had been Ken Knight who had picked up the puppy, and not Guy. She recalled once more the sight of him walking away earlier on, his arm round Nerissa. They had obviously been too engrossed in each other to realize poor Sheba had gone missing, which left Poppy right out in the cold.

10

THE following Monday Dave Hadden turned up.

"I'm sorry, but I don't have any sweaters for you," Poppy apologized, as soon as she had opened the door.

"Come off it! It's nearly Christmas! I got orders to fulfil."

"Orders?" she queried. He began to look rather shifty. "We had no arrangement like that. You bought my surplus sweaters — that's all. I'm afraid I've been ill, and now I have orders of my own to complete, from old clients. I'm sorry, Mr Hadden. I just don't have anything for you today. Perhaps in the New Year . . . "

"A fat lot of good, that is," he said angrily, looking and sounding belligerent. "I need a dozen or so right now, before Christmas."

"I'd no idea you took orders from

your market-stall," she snapped back, beginning to be annoyed. "Now, if you'll excuse me."

"Oh no, you don't. You've got a pile of sweaters on the table right there. I'll take them. You owe me . . . "

He tried to push past her into the house.

"Stay right where you are!" came the stentorian tones of a very angry Guy Devereau.

"You keep out of this, mister. This is between the lady and me."

With which he slipped past her into the kitchen. Guy followed, and as Dave Hadden turned uncertainly, Guy threw something on the table beside the neatly packaged sweaters. To Poppy's surprise, it was another one — pale pink patterned with cabbage roses in a tapestry design. It was one of the very ones Dave Hadden had 'taken off her hands' on an earlier occasion.

"Where did you get that, Guy?" she asked.

"South Molton Street, in the West

End," he told her, "where they're selling for ten times what he pays you!"

So this was the reason Guy wanted to see Dave Hadden! The latter turned a fiery red, but quickly recovered.

"Well, I'm damned, it's amazing what some of my customers get up to. Fancy 'er selling it on like that!"

"There's no 'her' about it," Guy went on with quiet fury. "The man who sold this and others to the boutique in question fitted your description exactly. You've been swindling this lady from the start! Saying they were for your market-stall!"

"Is this true, Dave?" Poppy asked quietly.

"We've all got a living to make," he protested, no longer bothering to deny anything.

"I don't believe I'm hearing this! You said you couldn't afford my usual price to sell on your *stall*! Then you go off to London and take far more profit than my bona fide retailers!"

"That's enterprise, ini'?"

"I've been selling them to you practically at a loss!"

"My 'eart bleeds."

"It very probably will," Guy told him with soft menace. Until now he had remained silent, listening to the exchange with interest. Now he seized Hadden by the collar and marched him towards the door. "Now just you get the hell out of here and don't ever come back."

He pushed him through the doorway, but not hard enough. The moment he was free, Hadden took a step backwards and lashed out with his elbow, catching Guy unawares in the solar plexis. He doubled up in pain and Hadden took advantage of this to make a grab for the sweaters on the table.

Guy straightened up in time to see what was happening, whereupon Hadden snatched up as many as he could and headed for the door — but Guy was quicker this time. Seizing the other man's shoulder, he twisted him round and slammed a fist into his face. The younger man recoiled, stunned but as yet unbeaten. He staggered out of the door, groaning and cursing, but still clutching his booty.

"I'll kill him," Guy muttered, after him like a shot.

"Guy, don't. Please! He's not worth it."

Her words were to no avail. Guy's hands clamped on Hadden's jacket shoulders and shook him in a bid to force him to let go. One by one the cellophane packets slipped from his grasp. With a roar of fury he bent to retrieve them.

"Oh no, you don't!" shouted Guy.

But when Hadden straightened up he was holding the loose piece of crazy paving in his fist. Lifting it high above his head and ignoring Poppy's screamed "No!", he dashed it down, catching Guy's temple. Guy slumped to the ground, unconscious.

"You've killed him! My God, you've killed him!" Poppy wept hysterically.

"It was self-defence," came the immediate disclaimer, but the words were tinged with fear. "You eard 'im. 'E threatened to kill me."

"He didn't mean it — you know he didn't!"

A groan came from the still form on the path.

"'E's all right, see? I'll be getting along. I guess you wouldn't consider a new deal, Poppy?"

"I don't ever want to set eyes on you again, Mr Hadden."

"Suit yourself."

She turned her attention to Guy, kneeling to cradle his head in her lap, and running her fingers over his handsome, beloved face.

"Oh Guy, I thought he'd killed you," she murmured, her own cheeks wet with tears. "Let's try and get you up, and I'll help you indoors?"

His reply was a series of groans and mutters but she had soon helped him to his feet, to lean on her as he staggered inside. There he sat down, head in hands, elbows on the kitchen table.

"I'd better call a doctor," she said swiftly.

He raised his head and scowled at her, barely restrained anger on his face. How unfair, when she had begged him not to get involved, was her first thought.

"Tell him to come to the Hall," he ordered coldly.

"Very well," she agreed, bewildered by his attitude, but doing as he asked.

When she returned to the kitchen he was on his feet — just.

"I'll drive you there," she told him.

"No need. I can walk — the same way I arrived."

"Don't be ridiculous, Guy — you may be concussed and, after two bouts of unconsciousness in so short a space of time . . ."

"So tell me about it," he said grimly, as if he would rather not know.

"I'm driving you back," she insisted.

"If you must, then."

Not a word was spoken all the way

there. She pulled up at the portico steps, where he slowly got out and staggered up the steps. Was Nerissa watching this strange scene from a window, she wondered?

She had hardly turned off the engine outside her cottage, when Robin drove past. He tooted his horn and shot off up the lane, obviously as concerned as she.

By why was Guy acting so strangely? He really was a moody man, she decided, as she retrieved the fallen packets of sweaters still strewn all over her path. After all, it really was not her fault what had happened, yet he had looked at her with positive hatred.

With her orders up to date she felt momentarily at a loss, till she remembered that she had been so busy lately she had hardly had time to do more than flick a duster round the cottage. She would clean the place up for Christmas.

She set to with a will, hoovering and sweeping, dusting and polishing, till every surface was clean as a new pin. Only she herself felt grimy, but she remedied this by running a bath and immersing herself in it for the next half hour, finishing by washing her hair and standing under the shower till she felt clean and fresh all over.

It grew dark early these days, and all she had planned was a quiet evening, with supper on a tray in front of the television. There was little point in getting dressed, so she belted a robe over a simple cotton nightdress and went down to make some supper.

She had barely begun, fighting down thoughts of Nerissa's cool, elegant hands soothing Guy's fevered brow, when there was a loud knocking on the door. Surely Dave Hadden hadn't waited till after dark to come back, she thought apprehensively.

"Open this door, Poppy," demanded a familiar voice.

Guy! Oh, why couldn't he leave her alone? She didn't know where she was with him any more. Renewed pounding on the oak panels of her kitchen door reminded her he was still there. If she didn't let him in, it sounded as though he was prepared to break the door down. Reluctantly she slid back the bolt and lifted the latch.

"What do you want, Guy?" she greeted him cautiously.

"To talk to you, of course. What the hell do you think?"

Yet earlier, he hadn't been able to get away fast enough!

"I don't see what we can possibly have to say to each other."

She planted herself firmly in the gap between door and jamb.

"Don't be ridiculous."

So saying, he moved her aside, walked in and closed the door.

"Guy, why can't you just leave me alone?" she asked, voicing her earlier thoughts.

"You really don't know the answer to that?" She looked at him warily. "Come through here, my girl, we have things to discuss."

Turning her with gentle firmness towards her sitting-room he urged her through the door, and almost pushed her down on to the soft cushions of the sofa. He followed her down, seizing her by the shoulders and towering over her.

"Why didn't you tell me?" he demanded, giving her a shake.

"Tell you what?" she asked guardedly.

"You're carrying my child, and you can ask me that?"

"Who told you?" she asked dully.

The only person she had confided in had been Tess. Had she told Robin who the father was, and had he then informed Guy? Oh, how could they?

"Nobody had to tell me. *I* told *Robin* and he thought I was probably right. But there's no probably about it. I've remembered everything, Poppy. It seems Hadden did me a favour, reversing the amnesia with that second blow. How could you not tell me? I even told you of my attitude to fatherhood, yet you still kept your precious secret. Why?"

"You know why, Guy — you're engaged to someone else — that's why!"

He looked amazed.

"You'd put the happiness of another woman before the security of your own child?"

"That's not how I see it, Guy."

Child or no child, she wanted no connection with a man who was in love with another woman, and who was not in love with her.

"Perhaps you'd like to explain just how you do see it."

"No, I wouldn't! Go away, Guy."

"That I'll never do, Poppy." He moved closer as if to prove the point. "You belong to me — you and our child. I'll never let you go."

"And what's Nerissa going to think of that?"

"Nerissa's out of the picture. I sent her packing last Thursday."

"Last Thurs . . . you mean after you left here with her, last . . . "

"Thursday, as I said. This is getting awfully repetitive, Poppy."

"But I thought you'd gone off to talk weddings."

"You thought wrong! I told Nerissa there was no future for us. We have absolutely nothing in common."

"How did she take that?"

"She threw hysterics! She ranted and screamed and threw things."

"Including the ring?"

"Strangely enough, no," he replied ironically, with the first hint of a smile. "Anyway, Dora came to ask how many for supper and caught the full force of Nerissa's quite shocking temper. I went off to apologize to my gem of a housekeeper, and, while my back was turned, Nerissa spitefully turned on Sheba and kicked her out through the French windows . . . "

"Poor Sheba — so that's what happened!"

"I didn't realize she was missing in that dreadful atmosphere. When you phoned, that was the first intimation any of us had of it. Dora replaced the receiver before you could hear the verbal abuse in the background for yourself."

Now she understood both that and Ken Knight's comments!

"Is she all right now?"

"I neither know nor care!"

Poppy frowned, puzzled. "I meant Sheba," she said eventually.

"Oh!" He grinned then. "Yes, she's fine — dogs are very forgiving."

"And Nerissa's gone?"

"She went that evening — thank God!"

"Did you propose to her, Guy?"

"No, I did not! I thought it rather odd — I certainly never saw her as wife material in Australia. And, in case you're wondering, no, I haven't slept with her, either."

That cheered Poppy up no end: she giggled.

"And I've been imagining you and her all lovey-dovey together up there!"

"You have thought about me, then?"

Poppy coloured, realizing what she had admitted.

"Occasionally."

"I've thought about you all the time, wondering what you were up to, and suddenly, would you believe it, shy about coming down to see you?"

"You? Shy?"

"That's what I said. I had to wait for an excuse — Hadden's visit — before I could pluck up the courage! When all the time," he went on angrily, "I had every reason in the world to spend my every waking — and sleeping — moment with you!"

"Not necessarily, Guy. Just because of one incident . . . "

"How can you say that? Oh, Poppy," he groaned, "you gave yourself to me so sweetly, that night. You crawled into my bed . . . "

"I did nothing of the kind! You dragged me there in a fit of delirium . . . "

"You stayed," he reminded her, "and I took your innocence. I'm sorry, it must have been awful for you . . . "

"It wasn't!" she said too quickly.

"Whatever — I'll make it up to you, I promise. I want to marry you, as quickly as possible . . . "

"No!"

"What do you mean — no?"

"You didn't mean to make me pregnant that night, did you?"

"Of course I damn well didn't!"

"Well, then. The fact that you did doesn't oblige you to marry me."

She had long since decided that if and when she did marry, it would be to someone she loved, and who loved her in return. There was no doubt Guy fancied her, but that was not enough for Poppy. It had to be love, or nothing.

"Why do you think I got rid of Nerissa?"

"Because you didn't love her, I suppose. That's no reason why I should fill the void she's obviously left — even though I inadvertently became pregnant with your child."

"There's every reason . . . "

The phone would choose that moment to ring! Poppy freed herself from Guy's restricting embrace to answer it.

"Robin!"

What on earth could he want right now?

"Are you all right?"

"Of course. Why?"

"I — er — I stayed for ages talking to Guy, calming him down. It seems his memory's returned, and I'm afraid your secret's a secret no longer . . . "

"I know."

"Anyway, he was hell-bent on coming straight back to see you, but I thought I'd talked him out of it — till he'd had longer to think. He was in a right old fury! I eventually left, but I'd hardly got halfway down the lane when I saw his Jaguar tearing down behind me, stopping at your place in a shower of dust."

Guy came to stand behind her. He lifted her silken mane of hair and began to inflict a series of kisses on the tender flesh of her nape. She squirmed away, but he caught her to him from behind, his lips tracing the outline of one shell-like earlobe.

"Say you'll marry me," he demanded softly as she tried to continue the conversation with Robin.

"Stop it, Guy," she begged, holding the mute button so that Robin would not hear.

"Not till you say you'll be my wife." He continued the torture till a helpless little sound escaped her throat.

"What was that, Poppy?" Robin enquired in alarm.

"Er, nothing — a frog in my throat. What were you saying, Robin?"

"I love you, Poppy Winters," Guy whispered hoarsely in her ear. "I love you, and I want to marry you. You're the most gorgeous," he punctuated each word with a teasing kiss, working slowly along her jawline till it became almost impossible to carry on the phone conversation, "wonderful, lovable . . . "

"What did you say?" she asked throatily.

"I say, Poppy, you do sound strange — perhaps I should come round and see for myself that things are okay."

"Things are very okay, Robin," she assured him, the happiness growing within putting a smile on her face, as she realized what Guy had said. He loved her! "In fact, they're more than okay. Guy's just asked me to marry him, and," she turned to the man in question, a flush on her cheeks, a sparkle in her eyes, "I've just accepted."

"You have?" both men asked simultaneously.

"I have," she assured them both happily.

Guy snatched the phone.

"I hope you're satisfied now, Robin, that I haven't strangled the wretched woman! Sorry, old boy. Can't talk now — things to do."

He returned the phone to its cradle. "And you," he informed Poppy purposefully, "are the person I intend to do them with for the rest of our lives. Come here, woman."

THE END

WITH SOMEBODY ELSE
Theresa Charles

Rosamond sets off for Cornwall with Hugo to meet his family, blissfully unaware of the shocks in store for her.

A SUMMER FOR STRANGERS
Claire Hamilton

Because she had lost her job, her flat and she had no money, Tabitha agreed to pose as Adam's future wife although she believed the scheme to be deceitful and cruel.

VILLA OF SINGING WATER
Angela Petron

The disquieting incidents that occurred at the Vatican and the Colosseum did not trouble Jan at first, but then they became increasingly unpleasant and alarming.

DOCTOR NAPIER'S NURSE
Pauline Ash

When cousins Midge and Derry are entered as probationer nurses on the same day but at different hospitals they agree to exchange identities.

A GIRL LIKE JULIE
Louise Ellis

Caroline absolutely adored Hugh Barrington, but then Julie Crane came into their lives. Julie was the kind of girl who attracts men without even trying.

COUNTRY DOCTOR
Paula Lindsay

When Evan Richmond bought a practice in a remote country village he did not realise that a casual encounter would lead to the loss of his heart.

A DANGEROUS MAN
Anne Goring

Photographer Polly Burton was on safari in Mombasa when she met enigmatic Leon Hammond. But unpredictability was the name of the game where Leon was concerned.

PRECIOUS INHERITANCE
Joan Moules

Karen's new life working for an authoress took her from Sussex to a foreign airstrip and a kidnapping; to a real life adventure as gripping as any in the books she typed.

VISION OF LOVE
Grace Richmond

When Kathy takes over the rundown country kennels she finds Alec Stinton, a local vet, very helpful. But their friendship arouses bitter jealousy and a tragedy seems inevitable.

ENCORE
Helga Moray

Craig and Janet realise that their true happiness lies with each other, but it is only under traumatic circumstances that they can be reunited.

NICOLETTE
Ivy Preston

When Grant Alston came back into her life, Nicolette was faced with a dilemma. Should she follow the path of duty or the path of love?

THE GOLDEN PUMA
Margaret Way

Catherine's time was spent looking after her father's Queensland farm. But what life was there without David, who wasn't interested in her?

HOSPITAL BY THE LAKE
Anne J urham

Nurse Marguer' Ingle y was always ready to bec personal y involved with her patients, to the despair of Brian Field, the Senior Surgical Registrar, who loved her.

VALLEY OF CONFLICT
David Farrell

Isolated in a hostel in the French Alps, Ann Russell sees her fiancé being seduced by a young girl. Then comes the avalanche that imperils their lives.

NURSE'S CHOICE
Peggy Gaddis

A proposal of marriage from the incredibly handsome and wealthy Reagan was e. ough to upset any girl — and Brooke Martin was no exception.